SLOW BURN

Julia stretched out alongside the stream. With her eyes closed, the sun and clouds danced patterns across her eyelids, sending her into a dreamlike state, until she heard Tony's footsteps. "What a wonderful day this has been," she said, although Julia knew that whatever way she expressed it, it would still be an understatement. "It sure beats any day I would have spent at the office."

"Oh, I don't know," Tony said, his voice a deep, sexy drawl. "I think playing doctor with you sounds pretty good. You can give me a check-up any time you want."

The words made her mouth go dry, then Julia heard the splash as Tony stepped into the water. She opened her eyes to a picture she was sure she would never forget.

Tony had taken off his boots and waded into the small stream. The afternoon breeze that cooled the day danced across the loose, windblown strands of his dark hair, adding a perfect frame to the laughing dark eyes. His smile was intimate, meant for her alone, and Julia found it impossible to look away as he approached her. When he stopped, only inches away, the smile in Tony's eyes changed, growing promising, intent, and smoldering. Julia sat up on the bank, yearning to touch him. Her lips already tingled in anticipation of his kiss . . .

<u>BOOK YOUR PLACE ON OUR WEBSITE</u>
<u>AND MAKE THE</u>
<u>READING CONNECTION!</u>

We've created a customized website just for our very special readers, where you can get the inside scoop on everything that's going on with Zebra, Pinnacle and Kensington books.

When you come online, you'll have the exciting opportunity to:

- View covers of upcoming books

- Read sample chapters

- Learn about our future publishing schedule (listed by publication month *and author*)

- Find out when your favorite authors will be visiting a city near you

- Search for and order backlist books from our online catalog

- Check out author bios and background information

- Send e-mail to your favorite authors

- Meet the Kensington staff online

- Join us in weekly chats with authors, readers and other guests

- Get writing guidelines

- AND MUCH MORE!

Visit our website at
http://www.pinnaclebooks.com

STARDUST

DIANA GARCIA

PINNACLE BOOKS
KENSINGTON PUBLISHING CORP.
http://www.encantoromance.com

For my father, Ronald Eugene Dennis. Everything I am or could ever hope to be begins with you.

And to Ryan Michael Garcia. For a little guy, you've got pretty strong shoulders. You and me, kiddo.

ONE

She'd been caught in the clouds for almost an hour and there was no sign of the storm ending anytime soon. The airplane plowed through the twisting, rolling mass of black, white, and gray, the wind sending the airplane sharply up or down at will. Julia removed her right hand from the throttle and wiped it on her jeans. She'd had more than enough.

Hoping to rise above the storm, she'd taken a gamble and gone all the way up to ten thousand feet—any higher and she would need oxygen. But gaining the extra altitude hadn't helped; she was still surrounded by clouds as far as she could see. And her airplane was getting low on gas from battling against the strong winds.

Julia's stomach felt the airplane's huge drop at the same time the altimeter registered the pocket of air. The small plane shuddered and recovered a few hundred feet below, leveling off only in time to be buffeted again by the high wind. A blinding flash of lightning exploded off of her left wingtip and Julia jumped in response, putting up her hand as if that could ward off the white blow. A crash of thunder echoed through the sky, chasing the lightning and rumbling away to leave only the pounding of the hard rain drowning out the static of the radio. Julia's hand was shaking as she returned it to the throttle. She hadn't meant to use her pilot's license for anything like this.

She would have to land soon—that much was clear. The Catalina Mountains loomed somewhere ahead in the mist, hidden in the blanket of clouds, and Julia wasn't about to try avoiding the sharp peaks in this storm. The thought of finding the ground below the cloudbank was almost as frightening, but her choices had run out; she wasn't going to fly her way out of this storm. Easing out the throttle, Julia sent the Cessna into a wide spiral toward the ground that lay somewhere below.

Julia circled downward, placing her trust in the airplane's instrument panel rather than in her own confused senses. When a narrow chimney of blue sky welcomed her at six thousand feet and promised a possible path to the ground, Julia tightened her circles around the opening in the clouds and sent up a quick prayer of thanks. If she was able to break out of the clouds early enough, she might be able to find a road she could land on, or at least a piece of flat ground. At this point, Julia wasn't wasting time looking for an airport—even an empty field would be fine. She just wanted to put the airplane on the ground. She would worry about getting it back out again after the storm had passed.

At a thousand feet, the rain pounding against the hull of the airplane turned to the soft ping of tiny shards of ice as hundreds of the white drops skittered across the windshield. Then suddenly Julia was beneath the storm, flying below the clouds, with the rain again her companion. The airplane soared low over the highway and Julia was able to take a long look at the ground below. The highway she followed was bounded on either side by fallow fields and there was only a single house in sight. Julia turned the airplane away from the highway, and headed in over the rich squares of farmland, trying to remember everything she had ever learned about soft-field landings.

Control yoke full aft. Full flaps. Minimum airspeed. Julia could almost hear her instructor calmly repeating the words as they stepped through the process. But they had never actually landed in a big muddy field during the flight lessons; it had all been theory until now.

The ground closed in fast, the tall stalks in the field brushing the wheels, whispering against the bottom of the plane. Julia flew lower until the wheels were nearly touching the rich ground in the field and it wasn't until the last second, when she was ready to set it down, that she saw the muddy strip a few feet beyond the field. A pair of torn windsocks waved a wild welcome. A runway when she needed it most. Thank God.

Her main wheels touched down at the beginning of the strip and the airplane slowed as the churned earth slapped against the plane beneath her feet. The oozing mud grabbed at the spinning wheels and tenaciously held on, bringing the plane to a stop so fast that Julia was flung forward against her seat belt. But she had made it without hurting either herself or the airplane. She could hardly believe it.

When the propeller came to a standstill, she switched off the engine and leaned her head back against the seat. The pounding of her heart was louder than the pounding of the rain.

It was the cold that finally forced her to move.

Since she had expected to be home long before dark, Julia had brought only a sweater and a light jacket, only enough to hold off the chill of her early morning flight. But the blowing thunderstorm had dropped the temperature dramatically and the jacket was of little help once the airplane was stopped and the heater was turned off. She was freezing and her fingers were numb. If she was ever going to make a try at finding the house, it had to be now. It took her three tries to unfasten the cold clasp of her seat belt.

The sky outside the airplane had faded to a dreary early evening and the rain had slowed to a soft, steady drizzle that draped long streamers of water across the airplane's windows and rattled against the metal hull like small pebbles. The light mist that had seemed to blanket the ground as she'd flown over it had thickened and closed in, wrapping itself around the airplane like a cold embrace. But above the crawling mist, Julia could still glimpse the stalwart neon wind socks waving brokenly in the gale. The wind socks would be her guides, her beacons in the darkness as she searched for the house she had seen from the air. Somewhere beyond the welcome of those orange wind socks waited warmth for Julia's cold fingers and possibly even a telephone.

The rain showed no sign of stopping, but Julia decided that she'd better make use of the little light she had left. She was going to get wet anyway, no matter how long she waited, and at least this way she wouldn't be walking in the dark, too. Resigning herself to the even colder air outside the airplane, Julia pulled up the handle to unlock the door. Pushing it open, she jumped out into the deluge.

The liquid ground swirled around Julia's feet like a huge, frigid puddle of chocolate milk and the thick mud sucked at her shoes, holding tighter to her Keds with every step as if determined that Julia would leave them behind to rest in the ooze. The sleeting rain was blowing almost sideways in the wind, and the heavy mist swept around her, invading her clothing, and repeatedly snaking a path of cold drops through her already soaked hair. The rain was even more thorough as it slithered beneath the dubious protection of her light jacket. Julia knew she would soon be as wet inside her clothes as she was outside. Her feet were soaked already.

By the time Julia reached the higher ground at the end of the runway and stepped up out of the mud, the rain had increased in determination, and large, fat drops spattered around her as they hit the ground. Julia's jacket was now soaked and completely useless, and the wet stuffing was packed into solid, small clumps that rested against her body and added more weight with every step. Julia stopped and wrung the water from the bottom of the jacket as she stepped up onto the long, watery lawn, but it did little good; she would probably be better off without the jacket altogether. But just ahead, Julia could see the adobe wall that marked the end of her frigid journey, and beyond the wall, the lights of a ranch house peeped reassuringly and promised shelter. Julia could see firelight reflected in the windows and a glimmer of welcome from beneath the porch door. She breathed a sigh of relief. Someone was home.

"Who are you and what are you doing on my property?" A man's voice leaped at her from the darkness beyond the wall. A huge, menacing shadow separated from the darker shadow of the house and stalked its way to the edge of the raised brick porch. Julia could only make out his shape, not his features, against the dusk, and it made her feel vulnerable. It was frightening.

She stumbled backwards, stepping into a shallow hole in the ground and almost slipped in the wet grass. Struggling to maintain her balance, Julia wiped the rain from her eyes with the wet sleeve of her jacket. The gesture was useless. The rivulets were immediately replaced by her dripping hair.

"I was caught in the thunderstorm and saw your house from the air," Julia shouted to be heard across the distance and above the storm. "I was lucky enough to find your runway to land on and I was hoping you could let me use your telephone. I promise I'll only bother you for a minute," she added haltingly. Julia had already changed her mind about seeking shelter. Maybe there was an old blanket in the airplane.

The shadow on the porch was silent. Julia could feel him watching her, judging her, deciding her fate on this cold, wet night.

She shivered with unease, her sense of discomfort growing with every second she waited for his answer. Perhaps the man was crazy, a hermit living out here all alone. After all, what kind of person would leave someone standing in the fury of a stormy night? Surely anyone inside the house would have heard the sound of the airplane's engine when Julia flew over before landing. The man had to know that she was telling the truth.

Maybe all the stories were true. Maybe she had made a big mistake by walking up to a stranger's house in the middle of nowhere, in the dark, all alone. No matter that she was cold and wet and might freeze during the night; at least if she stayed in the plane she would only be at the mercy of the elements, not at that of a lunatic. Maybe she shouldn't even go in to make the phone calls. Maybe she shouldn't go in at all.

"The gate to the wall is beneath the vines at the corner. You have to reach over the top and pull the latch from the inside to release it."

It wasn't much in the way of a polite invitation, and certainly not a very winning welcome, but Julia hesitated only a second before shaking off the effects of having seen too many horror movies. She was being ridiculous and letting her thoughts run away with her. Of course she would do the sensible thing and accept the man's offer; she really needed to make those phone calls. Besides, the man was probably no happier to let a wet stranger into his home at night than Julia was to go inside. If she could just manage to curb her wild imagination long enough to make a couple of telephone calls, everything was going to be fine.

Julia followed the wall to the far side, where she found the wooden gate hiding beneath a heavy layer of rain-drenched honeysuckle. When she reached over to find and release the latch, she disturbed the flowers and the sweet, clinging smell pushed the last thoughts of Chiller Theatre from her mind. There was absolutely nothing to be afraid of. This was not some grade-B movie. Julia lifted the old-fashioned wooden latch and stepped inside.

An enormous snarling animal leaped into her path.

Black hair stood high over a studded leather collar on its thickly muscled neck. Hungry black eyes watched Julia's every move and a fierce show of teeth bared by curling lips dared her to move. A menacing growl rumbled through the dog's giant body like a locomotive gaining steam. The dog was surely intended to guard the gates of hell and Julia was trapped with no escape. She didn't dare to run, was afraid no one would intervene should she scream, and was about to be torn limb from limb. It was her day to die.

"Down, Beast."

At the sound of his master's voice, the monster-dog dropped to his huge haunches. Julia was relieved but not at all reassured by the partial withdrawal. The animal still looked ready to spring at any second. He was a barely restrained killing machine.

"All the way down, Beast," the man commanded. The dog's intense gaze never left Julia's face as he eased his giant shoulders down onto the wet brick patio. His lip was still curled to best display his sharp, white fangs. Saliva dripped from his mouth.

"Come on inside the house," the man called

from the safety of the porch. "The dog is all show. He looks like a good guard dog, but he's not going to hurt you."

"His name is Beast?" Julia's voice squeaked as she asked the question. The dog's name was certainly fitting. A single snap from those enormous menacing teeth could probably take off her whole foot.

"You're out flying an airplane through weather like this, but you're afraid of a dog." The man sounded disgusted. "Well, you can stand out there in the rain all night if you want to, but I'm going back inside the house where it's warm. If you decide that you're cold out here, you can come on in. I've got a fire going."

If she was cold? Julia had been cold ever since she'd stepped out of the airplane and into a mud puddle the size of the Pacific Ocean. No, correction, she had been cold since she'd first flown into the storm that afternoon and discovered that the Weather Service had been damned wrong on their predictions. She was way past cold.

Julia warily watched the monster dog that lay directly across her path, blocking her way to the promise of a warm fire. There was still no sign of friendship. If Julia wanted to get past him and go inside, she would have to take her chances. And despite her earlier misgivings about the man, Julia definitely wanted to go inside. Not even the sight of the beast could keep her standing outside in the frigid rain for a minute longer. Inching her body close to the wall to keep as much space as she could between herself and the dog's teeth, Julia closed her eyes and took her first two steps beyond the gate.

The gate swung closed and latched with a bang.

Already tense from expecting fangs to sink into her leg, Julia almost screamed.

She opened her eyes and glanced at the dog. He was watching her, daring her into his domain, but as yet he hadn't moved. Still, Julia remained pressed against the wall as she waded through the wet grass the rest of the way to the porch.

She'd made it past the beast in the yard. Now, she had to brave the one in the house. Julia just hoped *he* didn't bite either.

She kicked off her muddy shoes at the edge of the flagstone steps and walked up onto the red brick porch. At the carved, wooden door to the house, Julia stopped. The door was pulled to, but not shut, and when she tapped lightly it swung open.

The man was standing in the kitchen, just inside the door. He turned at the sound and glared at her, giving Julia no doubt that she was unwelcome. "Hurry up. You're letting in the cold air! Here, take this towel and dry off." A towel flew at her head, wrapping the right side of her face in warmth. "Come inside and close the door."

The welcome rush of warm air from the doorway stopped Julia's caustic reply. Telephone and warmth, she reminded herself.

She stopped only long enough to wipe the water from her dripping hair before stepping inside the house. "I'm sorry for the inconvenience," she said, quickly pushing the door closed behind her. "If you could let me use your telephone for a few minutes, I'll make a couple quick calls to take care of things, and then I'll get out of your way."

The man was silhouetted against the light of the fire in the adjoining room, and Julia could see little beyond his shadow. It didn't make him appear any more welcoming. Julia shifted uncomfortably as she waited for his reply. The steady drip of water from the sleeves of her jacket filled the stillness.

"Wait here a minute and I'll find you something dry to put on," the man said finally. "The phone is in the other room, and you can't come inside my house like that."

"Don't go to any trouble," Julia called as he started to turn away. "I promise I'll be out of your way as soon as possible. I'm really sorry to bother you." She couldn't control the shiver as she said it.

The first sign of a smile lurked beneath the man's dark mustache. "It's no trouble and you're not bothering me," the man said. Then he turned down the hallway, leaving Julia standing alone in his warm kitchen. The evening had waned and the last cast of twilight barely made it in through the high old-fashioned windows that crossed the tops of the gleaming golden oak cabinets. Outside the house, the wind moaned its distress and sent a fury of rain lashing against the windows. A row of hanging copper pots shuddered and danced in the reflected red glow of the fire.

"Here." The man appeared out of the hall, holding a huge, blue towel and a long, white terrycloth bathrobe. When Julia took the two items, the man motioned to a closed door to her right. "That's the laundry room. You can change in there and drop your clothes in the dryer." He pressed a switch on the wall and, as the kitchen flooded with light, Julia got her first good look at her beast.

His shadow had seemed enormous when she'd first seen him on the porch, like some kind of mythological creature, but the man wasn't really so tall. He was about six feet even, only a half dozen inches or so above Julia's own height. He was strongly built with a muscled body, but not heavy, and nothing had gone to fat. Strong, wide shoulders filled the doorway. Dark hair showed beneath the open neck of a blue chambray work shirt and it was impossible to not want to stare. The dark hair appeared again on a strong chin that had probably been a few days without shaving and curled lightly over cheeks dented with humor. The man's mustache had survived a much longer time and was thick and full above the line of his lips. His nose reminded Julia of the Roman conquerors, ruining the perfect symmetry of his face, keeping the lines from true beauty. Instead, the nose and the heavy brows that furrowed over the man's deep brown eyes gave the face character—and made it overwhelmingly masculine.

His dark eyes fairly snapped with quick intelligence, with traces of warmth and, perhaps, humor. And when the man smiled, his perfect teeth flashed against his tanned skin and dark mustache.

He was completely gorgeous.

Julia had to force her gaze away from his face, although she was certain he had already seen her staring. She usually wasn't one to be jealous, but the woman who owned that beautiful kitchen and curled up next to those blue-black whiskers every night was one lucky lady.

Making a quick escape, Julia stepped through the door the man had indicated and into a large laundry room that wasn't as pretty as the kitchen, but it was just as well organized. Along the far wall was a door leading to a pantry stocked with enough canned goods to see the couple through a long, cold winter—something they'd certainly never see in this part of the Southwest. Not a couple, but a family, Julia amended as she saw the piles of neatly folded clothes waiting beside the ironing board. There was a pile set out for the husband, a pile for a boy and a pile for the wife.

So much for any small hope she might have had.

Her teeth chattering, Julia started removing her wet socks, peeling them off her cold feet and wiggling her toes until she could feel the tingle of returning blood. The wet jeans were next and the rough material chafed her enormous goosebumps as Julia slithered out of the clinging material. After she pulled off her soaked sweater and T-shirt, the air brushed her wet skin and set her shivering again. Gratefully, Julia slipped her arms into the warmth of the heavy white robe she'd been given, and its thick, terrycloth folds covered her body from ankle to chin, gradually warming away the goosebumps and ending the shivers that were shaking through her. Finally warm enough to move, Julia opened the dryer and tossed her wet clothing inside. She tightened the belt of the robe and turned the small silver knob on the dryer until the soft rumble of the motor filled the room. By the time she finished her telephone calls, her clothes would be dry and she could be on her way. A night in the airplane wouldn't be so bad if she wasn't wet. Maybe she could borrow an umbrella.

When she had cleaned up the mess in the laundry room, Julia toweled her hair dry and tried to tuck at least some of it neatly behind her ears. Without a mirror it was impossible to tell how it looked. She just hoped it wasn't sticking out in every direction. She pulled open the door to the kitchen, and was startled to find the man standing right outside. She hadn't heard a sound.

His dark gaze ran over Julia, from her wet hair to her bare toes, obviously not trying to hide the fact that he was taking it all in, but not lingering long enough to be insulting either. Julia knew that it was silly to feel shy in such an unflattering outfit; the robe was bulky and long and less revealing than a comfortable pair of sweats. Still, she couldn't help but feel undressed. When the man made no comment, Julia found herself wondering if he found the view attractive or objectionable.

Without speaking, the man held out her now-clean, wet Keds, and Julia tossed them into the dryer with the rest of her clothes. When she turned back, the man was gone.

Tony took a long drink from his glass of water as he listened to Dr. Julia Huerta close her flight plan with the Phoenix airport. And on her next telephone call, she left a short message with someone to cancel her office appointments for the following day. Tony's hand began to relax around the fragile glass. Until that moment, he hadn't been sure what to believe about the woman's surprise arrival. Accidentally landing an airplane on *his* ranch sure stretched the imagination. Tony had figured he'd been found again and the thought hadn't made him happy.

But, despite the odds, it was starting to look like this lady was exactly who she claimed to be—a doctor caught in a thunderstorm on her plane trip home. Either way, Tony was going to have plenty of time to find out, because there was no way that she was going to get home tonight. The weather looked as though it might keep raining all night and it already was damned cold outside and likely to get colder before dawn. Despite her offer, Dr. Julia wouldn't be leaving Tony's home anytime soon.

He studied her perfect profile as she talked on the phone, watching her soft, gentle smile flash in her lovely, expressive face. She was almost too pretty, all rain-washed and clean, almost too approachable, sitting there in the window seat—his own favorite place to sit, and wearing his bulky bathrobe that was much too big for her. The flickering play of the firelight deepened the shadows of her cheekbones and highlighted the expressive, gray eyes that Tony had already seen flash with both fear and fury. She was a woman of grand passions— he was sure of it—and the thought did nothing to ease his growing desire.

"Thanks for taking care of them for me, Joan," she said into the telephone. "It will only be for tonight and I'll be home as soon as this storm lets up. I'll stop by your place tomorrow when I get in."

Even her voice was perfect—sexy, soft and husky, just the way he liked it. In fact, Tony had noticed that everything about Julia Huerta seemed to be just the way he liked it. Everything about her caught his attention. When he'd first seen her standing outside the wall, waiting in the tall grass of the yard, with her wet clothes plastered against her body and her dark bangs dripping into her eyes, he hadn't even known who she was yet, and had truly imagined her an intruder bent on taking away his solitude. But she had still touched something inside of him. It was as though this woman had dropped from the sky just for him.

Tony's mouth tightened. He had been without a woman, any woman, for too damned long. That was all. He would get over it soon enough. He stood up and headed into the kitchen to make a pot of coffee. At least it would give him something to do besides stare at the beautiful doctor sitting in his living room. He wasn't going to be getting any sleep tonight anyway.

By the time his guest finished making her telephone calls and walked in to join him in the kitchen, Tony already had a steaming mug of coffee in his hand. "Were you able to find someone to watch your kids for the night?" With Julia's dark hair tousled and whatever makeup she might normally wear washed away by the rain, she looked young enough to be a kid herself.

"It's not kids, I'm afraid," she said. "Just a few spoiled cats who want their dinner. My neighbor feeds them for me whenever I go out of town." Julia ran her fingers through her dark, wet hair, pushing the curls from her eyes. A drop of water escaped the curls and raced a path down her cheek, disappearing into the neck of her bathrobe. Tony looked away.

"That's nice that you have someone who can fill in for you," he said. "I'm having coffee. Want a cup to help warm you up?"

"Oh . . . thanks, but I really should check on my

clothes and get out of your way here. It sounds like the storm has almost blown over."

A huge crash of thunder exploded overhead, shaking the walls of the house and making a lie of her words. The timing was perfect. They both laughed.

"Your clothes won't even be close to dry yet," Tony said, "and the storm doesn't show any sign of stopping soon. Why don't you just plan on staying in my guest room and you can have breakfast with us in the morning before you leave."

The doctor's smile faded. Her even, white teeth chewed uncertainly on her full bottom lip. Tony felt a stirring he hadn't felt in years.

"I'm embarrassed to say this," she said, looking up at him with a soft smile, "especially while I'm standing here wearing your wife's bathrobe, but I'm afraid I don't even know your name. And somehow it doesn't feel right to just show up at your door, start borrowing things—including your guest room—and then expect to be served breakfast in the morning."

"The bathrobe is mine," Tony said. "So you have no one else to thank for it but me. In fact, it's just me, my daughter and my son around here, so anything else you want to borrow is all right with me, too." He set the coffee cup on the kitchen counter and stepped into a pair of loafers waiting by the back door. "I'll be right back," he said. "I'm going to bring in some more firewood from the garage."

He had almost made it out of the room before Julia stopped him with a soft touch of her hand on his arm. Tony turned to find her lovely gray eyes studying him and waited for the questions that he was sure were coming. This was it.

"You still forgot to tell me your name," she said.

Tony hesitated, but stuck with the truth. "Tony. Tony Carrera."

"It's a pleasure to meet you, Tony. I'm Julia Huerta."

"I know." Tony accepted the small, outstretched hand she offered, covering its warmth with his own. Her hands were strong, but so very soft. "And believe me, Julia," he said, "the pleasure is all mine."

Tony smiled as he turned away toward the door. There hadn't been a flash of recognition when she heard his name. Not a sign.

Maybe he'd been gone long enough after all.

TWO

Julia restlessly prowled through Tony's living room, studying the array of rustic art that covered the walls, running her fingers across gleaming brass accents, and admiring an eclectic display of knickknacks that filled an enormous cabinet with floor-to-ceiling shelves. It was a daunting collection.

There were small, serious statues that posed in groups and stared back at Julia with peaceful expressions on their wise, ancient faces. There was an assortment of Asian carvings with heavily slanted eyes and wide grins that had been etched into a beautiful red teak wood, and each carving was more detailed than the last. There were even stone pieces Julia recognized as representing the ancient gods of the Incas. Four long shelves were filled front to back and almost to overflowing with the crowd of knickknacks, but none of the figurines looked like something you would find in a cheap tourist shop. Each had a special beauty, an inherent value that even the crowding of the pieces couldn't disguise. Julia was certain that each item on the shelves was one of a kind.

In the back row of the middle shelf, the golden shine of a dragon's tail caught Julia's attention first. It was a mythological creature with wings that were a few inches long and golden fire spouting from its mouth. And when Julia crouched down to admire the dragon, she also saw a double-sided wooden picture frame that had been hidden behind the sparkling creature. The simplicity of the frame was what attracted her attention. It was not the type of item you would expect to find amid such an eclectic collection of art, and the wood was cracked on one side and undusted as if its very existence had been forgotten.

Even when Julia held them up to the light, the photos in the frame were dim and faded, but the one on the left was unmistakably Tony, although he looked only a little older than a teenager. On the other side of the double frame was a young, dark-haired girl with a brilliant smile.

"This ought to hold us for a while."

Julia hurried to set the picture back on the shelf and when she pulled her hand out, the long sleeve of her robe knocked over the green and gold dragon, breaking the tail into two crystal pieces. Julia stared at the two jagged pieces for a long moment before finally willing herself to pick them up. She was horrified, but there was really no choice; she was going to have to admit what she had done. Putting the inevitable off for as long as possible, Julia waited until Tony had dropped the logs into the woodbox.

Julia opened her hand. "I'm afraid I broke something from your shelves," she said. "I know that I shouldn't have touched it, and I'm terribly sorry. I would be happy to pay you whatever you think it's worth."

For some reason the offer made him laugh. "No, that won't be necessary," Tony said. Crossing to her side, he took the two pieces and returned them to their place on the shelf. "None of that stuff is important. It's just some things I collected to remind me of places I've been, and it'll remind me again just fine with some glue. Don't worry about it."

It amazed her that she had ever been frightened of him. Tony's kindness was there in his voice, in his manner, and in his laughter when he finally dropped his guard. It seemed as though he had tried to keep the kindness hidden at first and tried to keep his distance from her, but finally he had seemed to relax, and his good humor was contagious. Julia liked watching Tony's expressive face; he looked like a man who smiled a lot, a man who enjoyed life to the fullest.

She was staring again, and Julia could feel the flush rising in her cheeks as she yanked her gaze away. She struggled for small talk, grasped for unimportant words to fill the silence.

She couldn't think of a thing to say.

Tony saved her. "It's getting late and you must be exhausted. You've probably had a long day what with flying through the storm and all," he said. "I know something like that would sure wear me out. So since we both agree that you're going to be staying the night, why don't I show you to your room?"

He didn't wait for her answer about staying, and if he was laughing at her for the staring and the blushes, he at least had the grace to wait until he had turned away, and Julia was grateful for that. On the other hand, a man who looked like Tony was probably well used to being stared at. Good thing, too, since staring seemed to be all Julia was capable of around him.

At the end of the long hall, the guest room Tony showed her to was comfortable, quaint, and old-fashioned like the rest of the house that Julia had seen. Colorful quilts decorated the pale walls and more quilts were layered on the bed, giving cozy warmth to the off-white room. Sprigs of dried flowers were everywhere, bringing a touch of spring into the room, and a giant bouquet of dried lavender hung above the bedroom door, the long purple strands filling the air with the sweet memories of summer. Beneath their feet, hardwood floors shone golden in the lamplight, and half a dozen rag rugs, like those Julia's aunts once made, lay scattered about.

"Your home is really beautiful," Julia said, running her fingertips lovingly over the antique cherry wood dresser. "I love all the antiques you managed to find. There's just something about owning something with a long history that makes it special. I keep saying that I'll replace my department store furniture with the real thing someday, but I never seem to get around to it." Julia was trying to keep her tone light and conversational, trying to keep herself from embarrassing them both with this sudden infatuation, but when she turned, their gazes collided and Julia suddenly no longer felt alone in her desire.

Tony's heated dark gaze swept over her from toes to hair again, just as it had outside the laundry room, but this time, there was no doubt in Julia's mind that Tony approved of the way she looked in his robe.

It was a heady feeling.

But instead of acting on the desire she thought they shared, Tony took a step backward into the hall, putting the distance of the raised doorway between them. His hand against the doorframe seemed to hold him there, braced away from her. Julia wet her lips. Her mouth was dry with disappointment that he hadn't come closer. It was impossible, of course, but she'd hoped. "Good night, then," Julia whispered.

Of course, the desire she felt was absurd—she didn't even really know Tony. Maybe it had just been so long since she had been around an attractive man that her hormones were raging. As Julia closed the door to the lovely bedroom, shutting out the temptation to follow him back down the long hall, she decided she was going to have to try dating a little more often.

Outside the comfortable bedroom, the night was wild and storm-tossed and the determined wind rose and fell, crying out its complaints against the low tumbling clouds that swept in with it. And beneath the hand-stitched quilts and comforters, Julia tossed just as restlessly in her sleep, as unsettled as the night around her. But it was not the crying of the storm that disturbed her, it was something she had never heard before.

Somewhere, from deep within her dreams, a new song had called out to her, awakening Julia with soft music that curled around her, pulling at her to come with it, taking her to flow along with the gentle melody that sprinkled down through her dreams like a soft summer rain. The new sound drifted through the wild night like a part of the storm, rising and falling with the wind. But it wasn't the storm; it was more the aftermath, the renewal, the blessing of the rain on the parched land. Then the haunting song broke apart and tumbled out of reach, blowing through the dark sky, softer and softer, until it disappeared completely.

Half awake, Julia sat up in bed, pushing down the covers until a rush of cool air brought reality and awareness. She forced herself awake and waited, listening for the song she had heard in her dreams. She was groggy and confused and unsure that the sound had even been real, but it had seemed real. It had seemed so much a part of the windswept night.

Julia lay awake for a long time, listening for the song to return, but it was gone or had never existed. There was nothing to hear beyond the sound of the wind dancing through the trees, the pitch and toss of a fretful rain and, now and again, the mournful lowing of faraway cattle. At last Julia turned over in the bed and settled her head back against the pillows. She turned the alarm clock to face her and yawned as she saw the numbers shining through the darkness. She'd been asleep for less than an hour.

She was just beginning to slide back into dreams when the haunting music began to rise again with the rise of the wind in the trees. This time, Julia leaped out of the bed before even the first few notes of the song had a chance to float away and disappear. Softly, quickly, she opened the bedroom door and stepped out into the hallway, smiling as the song became clearer. It was indeed the song of sprinkling rain, but it was being played on a guitar.

Tony heard the familiar squeak of the old porch door as it opened and his fingers stilled against the guitar strings, the melody slipping away.

"Please don't stop playing," Julia said softly. "I heard the music outside and had to find it. I don't want to interrupt."

She'd stopped just outside the screen door and the halo of her hair was framed in the porch light. She looked like an angel in a shapeless white gown. Tony almost laughed at Julia's request to keep playing, because she was the very reason he was outside in the first place. He always played when he was frustrated, although usually he was frustrated in a whole different way.

"I didn't mean to wake you," he said. "I didn't think you'd be able to hear me if I came out here."

Julia shook her head and her wayward brown curls fell in her eyes. He wanted to push his fingers through their silk.

"It's been a restless night," she said. "All the excitement, I guess. I couldn't really get to sleep."

Tony ran his fingers over the guitar strings, softly mimicking the sound of the water relentlessly dripping from the roof. Once he got the rhythm, he could hit it with almost every note. He'd had a lot of practice at playing the rain. "I couldn't sleep, either," he said. If Julia heard the irony behind the words, she gave no sign.

Julia crossed the porch and took a seat up on the rail, looking out over the wet landscape. Her smile was soft when she turned back to him.

"You're playing the fall of the rain, aren't you?" Tony nodded. "That was the sound I first heard, the sound that woke me up. It was so perfect that I wasn't really sure that I'd heard it, that the song didn't belong to the storm. I thought it was part of a dream. I've never heard anyone play guitar like that. Where did you learn?"

Tony had heard people say all kinds of things as compliments, but being part of Julia's dreams was surely the best. He wrapped his arms around the neck of his guitar, his oldest friend. He'd had fancier guitars with prettier paint jobs, but the scarred twelve-string had been with him through all the tough times, from the very beginning, and it had never done him wrong. "I started playing a long time ago," he said, "back when my dad and a bunch of his friends used to play in any old club that would have them. As a teenager, I started tagging along all the time, and after they got tired of making me run errands, they started letting me play. I think they felt sorry for me."

Julia leaned back against the weathered wooden post of the porch and Tony's old robe blessed him by parting a few inches from ankle to mid-thigh. Tony stared at the narrow view of creamy muscled calves and slender knees that the parted robe revealed. When Julia said that she was sure he was very good, he almost choked. He'd forgotten what they were discussing.

"But instead you decided to move out here and become a rancher."

Back in safer territory. Tony resolutely returned his gaze to Julia's face. "Inside, I really always was a rancher. I went and lived the wild life for a while, like all kids want to I guess, but I never did care very much for it. In the big cities, I found that the people are different and their values are different.

"When it came time to settle down I didn't want to do my settling in one of those big cities, and I'd had enough anyway. I figured since ranching had raised me right, it would do all right by my kids, so we packed up and moved back home." Tony stopped and raised his hand. "But, hey, you already know all about my life. You've seen my house, and my bathrobe, you've even met my dog," Tony added. "Tell me some stories about Julia Huerta instead."

Julia shrugged. "There's not really that much to tell," she said. "I'm afraid that my life isn't very interesting. I never lived the wild life and I never learned to play the guitar."

Tony ducked his head to hide his smile. She sure looked interesting to him. "So far, all I know is that you live in Phoenix, that you fly airplanes and that you're a doctor. This should be easy. There has to be more to it than that."

"Nope. That's about it," Julia said. "I live with three cats in a small apartment in Scottsdale and I own an even smaller medical office in Phoenix. I put in far too many hours at South Phoenix Hospital and fill in any gaps of time at a clinic in Buena Vista. It keeps me pretty busy, but since I'm the first to admit that I have absolutely no life away from the office, it doesn't really bother me."

"When you were growing up, did you always know you would be a doctor?"

"No," Julia said and she laughed. "Growing up, I had no idea what I wanted to do. I managed to make it through college and started out with a career in social work for lack of a better idea, but after a few years I decided the lifestyle wasn't for me. As a social worker, I felt like I was hanging on the fringe of the important decisions. I had to follow someone else's set of rules and that wasn't what

I wanted; I needed to be more involved. I wanted to be able to really change things, and to do that I knew I had to reach the people that the social system didn't reach, the ones who were left outside the door. One day I quit social work, went back to school for a medical degree, and here I am."

She said it so simply, as if it had been handed to her, but to Tony it sounded like Dr. Julia had worked awfully hard to get where she was. Silent again, she stared out into the darkness and he used the opportunity to stare at her. Then Julia shivered and pulled the huge robe closer around her neck. "That wind has a real bite to it," she said, turning toward him on the rail. "Aren't you cold?"

The view of her leg disappeared and Tony sighed for the loss. "I don't think I'll ever be cold again," he mumbled, but he didn't think she heard him. Then he looked up at her and held out his hand. "Come sit over here by me. Against this wall you'll be out of the wind."

Julia accepted his hand and sank to a seat beside him on the bricks, warming Tony's shoulder with the brush of hers and stretching out her legs so her pink-tipped toes just reached the tops of his shoes. They fit so well together. Tony was sure that no one's touch had ever felt so natural.

The wind had blown Julia's hair into her eyes, and now she fumbled with it, pushing the curls away and tucking the longer strands behind her ears. She smiled ruefully when she saw him watching. "Usually I keep my hair up and out of my face," she said. "I can't stand it when it gets like this."

He could stand it.

Tony gave in to temptation and slid his hand through the soft, clinging curls. The fall of her hair was like a brush of silk against the work-roughened skin of his hand, like cool water against his fingertips. Beneath his touch, Julia stilled, her gray eyes growing wide and serious as her gaze met his. Tony enjoyed the sensation of drowning in those eyes.

"You have the most beautiful hair," Tony said. "You should leave it down all the time, and windblown, just as it is right now. I love the way it curls right here—against your cheeks." One short ringlet wrapped itself around his finger, seeming to dare him to draw closer to her: to her shining hair, soft skin, and kissable lips.

Somehow he managed to resist the temptation. Lost in her eyes, he managed to pull back. Fate had placed her in his arms, but Tony had only just talked her into sitting next to him and he didn't want to ruin that first step. He took in a deep breath of the cold night air and returned his attention to the stranger instead of the woman he already seemed to know. "So, from social work you turned to medicine, and now you spend your time flying around the country saving lives."

Julia laughed. "Hardly anything that heroic, I'm afraid," she said. "Actually, I'm in family practice and most of the time, my emergencies amount to ear infections, sore throats and rashes. At the clinic in Buena Vista, we give a lot of shots and lectures on family planning."

"But now you feel like you're making a difference."

Julia nodded. "No one in America can really understand how difficult life can be in the border towns. The simplest necessities are impossible, and when families fall through the cracks, there is no social system in place to help.

"Sometimes these people have traveled thousands of miles to find work, thousands of miles to find a way to survive, and when they come north, they bring pregnant wives and sick children. Then they finally reach the American border and they're confronted with a reality they aren't prepared for. Many are simply trapped. They can't go home to war and certain poverty, but they can't cross the border. And they don't have enough money for food, much less medical care.

"So we try to help a few of these families. And if they can pay in animals or fruits and vegetables, then the clinic gratefully accepts the donation and passes the food on to the next hungry family who comes through the door. It builds a sense of community and everyone saves their pride by being allowed to pay what they can."

It had been a very long time since Tony had heard anyone speak with such conviction about their beliefs, had seen anyone actually put into practice the values they preached to others. "Are there other doctors working at the clinic with you?"

"There are some, but not nearly enough. All the work there is done by volunteers and everyone is so busy these days that it's almost impossible to get a firm commitment from people." She shrugged. "But there are six of us who come in regularly, and somehow we manage to keep the clinic open on most of the weekends."

"Just on the weekends?"

"It's all we can afford on the donations we get.

Even so, sometimes the donations and the grants aren't enough to cover all of the clinic's expenses and we end up pooling our own money to make up the difference. Which brings me," she said with a smile, "to the reason I keep my day job in Phoenix when I'd rather live on a ranch like this in the middle of nowhere. It's wonderful that you have all of this space to yourselves. Is it just you and your kids out here?"

"Mostly. We have a housekeeper that drives out twice a week for the real housecleaning, and I have some ranch hands that work around here once in a while, but only my foreman has a place on the property."

"I don't remember seeing another house when I was flying over today. I guess I missed it in the storm."

"You wouldn't have seen his house if you were coming from Buena Vista. My foreman's place is on the other side of the mountain."

Julia looked at Tony as though she suspected him of lying. "You have to be kidding. That mountain must be over five miles away."

"That sounds about right," Tony said. "It takes a lot of land to run cattle in Arizona. For starters, you have to have enough brush to feed each cow, and enough water to keep them alive, and that's not easy to do during the dry season. In fact, most of the ranches around this area are pretty large."

Julia whistled softly. "I'll bet you could ride a horse all day and never reach the end of your own property. Now that's the kind of wide-open space I'd like to own, enough space to really get away from it all. I think I would put a six-foot fence all the way around and build my house right in the center."

"A walk like that would be awfully daunting to your patients."

"Well, of course I would have to be terribly rich, too," Julia said. "Then I could open the clinic in Buena Vista full time during the week and stand in the middle of my endless land on the weekends." She sighed. "You see, there's the proof: Money *can* buy happiness."

"Don't bet on it," Tony said. He pushed away from the wall and stood up. "That's a lie that all the world believes, but it's not true. Sometimes all the money in the world can't buy what's most important. I've seen people throw their whole lives away reaching for the golden ring and end up with only empty air to keep them warm at night. My ex-wife was sure she was missing something and she had to go find it. Well, she found the money, but she still doesn't realize what she lost."

Tony leaned against the fence, his attention far away. Julia crossed the porch to stand beside him and ran her hand gently down his arm. "I'm sorry," she said.

Tony shook his head and covered Julia's hand with his own. His thumb lightly stroked over the pulse at her wrist. "I don't know why I even mentioned it; I only care because of my kids," he said softly. "When their mother left, it was in both body and spirit, and it's hard for them to understand that she doesn't want to be here while they're growing up. For me, its all water that went under the bridge a long time ago and I wouldn't want to go backward even if I somehow could.

"In the evenings, when I stand out here with my kids, watching the sun setting over those mountains and the colors of the day's end flooding the sky, I forget I've ever been anywhere else, ever done anything else. I'd swear I'd always been here, living this life on this ranch. And I'm old enough to know that I wouldn't want to be anywhere else. This is where I was meant to be, and I can't see anything ever changing that."

"That's beautiful, Tony. You sound like a poet."

Tony groaned and turned towards her. His hands traced a light path across her shoulders and down her arms. "Trust a woman to say something like that," he said. "They've always got to make things mushy."

Julia laughed and leaned into his tender touch. Tony's hands were warm and strong, muscled with hard work, and wise and knowing as they stroked the tension from her shoulders. "I didn't mean it as an insult," she said. "I just meant that you have a wonderful way with words."

"I'll settle for having a wonderful way with horses," Tony said. "Because that's what really counts around here."

Tony was so tall that Julia had to look up to see his face in the shadows. The size difference made her feel petite and desirable—and reminded her how very naked she was beneath the thick bathrobe. Tony's lightest touch on her arms sent a thrill through her body and made her desire things Julia knew she shouldn't want and couldn't have. She wanted to lean into Tony, absorb his heat, have him share the desire that inflamed her.

"Come with me to the barn and I'll show you."

Julia was sure her face flamed bright red with the thought that crossed her mind. It took her a full minute to follow the conversation. She had to slip out of reach of his touch to be able to answer. "I'd love to go out to the barn and see your horses," she said. Thank goodness it was dark; she prayed it hid her flushed skin. "Just give me a minute to change into my clothes."

"Do you have to?" Tony's question was soft and beguiling, barely reaching her ears, but Julia heard it; Julia felt it. The heat that had infused her face flared through her entire body, setting her nerve endings singing. She didn't dare look at Tony when she answered. "We wouldn't want the horses to get the wrong idea," she joked weakly. The words felt thick in her throat.

He held the kitchen door open for her and Julia had to brush against him to get inside the house. The attraction positively jolted through her. Never in her life had she felt so aware of a man—aware of his presence and his touch. Never had she found herself praying for more. Julia was almost thankful for Beast's deafening arrival when the dog raced to the door to greet them, his bark roaring through the room. Staying away from the animal's sharp teeth gave her something to concentrate on besides the way Tony filled out his jeans.

"I promise, he's not going to hurt you," Tony repeated for the second time, petting Beast's giant head and trying to convince Julia to come out from behind the wooden door and do the same. "He'll probably even grow to like you if you give him a chance."

"Yeah," Julia agreed. "He'd like to eat me for breakfast if I gave him a chance." Still she went so far as to put one hand out from behind the safety of the door and let the big dog sniff it. Beast's nose actually touched her bare skin. Twice. Surely that amount of courage was all anyone could reasonably ask.

When Beast lost interest and walked away, Julia counted herself lucky that all ten fingers still remained. Only when she was sure the dog was gone did she come out. Then she made a dash for the safety of the laundry room and closed the door behind her.

Her jeans and sweater were dry and warm and felt good to slip into, but her tennis shoes were still damp and were hard to pull on. They squeaked as Julia stepped onto the tiled floor of the hallway and with each step she took towards the kitchen. The overhead light in the room was off, but the glow of the fire from the den sent flickers of light to lead her way. In the kitchen, Julia found Tony silhouetted against the tiny, white light of the refrigerator bulb. The monster-dog was nowhere in sight.

"Catch."

A shadow flew at her from across the room. She wasn't ready. Without thinking, Julia shrieked and put up her hands. Somehow, she managed to catch the apple before it fell to the floor.

"Good catch," Tony said. He didn't sound as though he meant it.

"Hey, it's dark in here," Julia defended herself. "And I didn't know it was coming. Anytime you want to take me on in the daytime, then we'll see who can catch. But I'm better with a baseball than an apple."

"Yeah, yeah. I've heard it all before. You probably catch like a girl."

"I do not," Julia answered hotly, then she stopped and considered. "Well, okay, maybe I do catch like a girl. I am a girl."

Tony turned from the refrigerator and pushed the door closed with his foot. "I noticed that," he said. His voice was low and sexy. He stood only a few inches away from her in the darkened kitchen, and Julia could feel the caress of his gaze, a gaze that mirrored the burn she'd been fighting all evening. A burn she didn't want to fight anymore.

She was squeezing the apple so hard that there was juice on her fingertips.

Tony reached out his hand to her, opening his arms in a single questioning gesture. He took no step toward her, leaving the decision up to Julia, leaving her to turn away if she wished. But there was no question in Julia's mind as she stepped into Tony's arms for the welcome of his kiss.

It was possession, pure and simple. His mouth on hers, the brush of his mustache against her lips, the feel of his breath, the electric touch of his tongue as it danced with hers. Tony's kiss was potent and searing, hot and taking, and left Julia dizzy with the promise of carnal delights beyond her imagination. The forgotten apple fell from her fingers and plummeted to the tile floor with a dull thump. Julia's hands moved up to tangle in Tony's hair, and to dreamily trace the taut muscles of the shoulders and arms that held her so gently, so tightly.

The feel of Tony's body pressed intimately against her own was the stuff fantasies were made of, and this was a fantasy that Julia ached to fulfill, one desire she wanted to have come true. When Tony trapped her with her lower back against the countertop, Julia welcomed the imprisonment with a sigh of satisfaction, welcomed the feel of him, the weight of him, resting between her legs, welcomed Tony's knowing hands as they traced her body . . . and slipped away.

He'd stopped. The fog blew away from her mind when Tony ended the soul-shattering kiss, ended the touch. When Julia opened her eyes, their gazes met in a single moment of clarity and understanding. There was no need for words to know that he wanted what she wanted. And no need to speak to know that they were in Tony's home, in his kitchen with his children nearby—and that it was an unacceptable risk. For a moment neither of them moved to break away. They stared at one another, continuing the intimate contact without a touch, both still breathing hard. Tony finally broke the moment, pulling away his gaze and stepping back so that feet rather than inches separated them. He bent down to pick up the bruised apple from the floor. Taking Julia's hand, he opened her fingers and pressed the apple against her palm. "It's getting late," he said softly, releasing her hand. "Guess we should go see those horses before they fall asleep."

Julia's laugh was shaky as she followed him out the door.

THREE

Somewhere behind the angry clouds, the yellow moon was nearly full and gave the clouds and the dark sky an eerie, incandescent glow. The smell of rain still blew across the wet ground, but the drops had stopped falling, and dripping water kept rhythm only from the water-soaked leaves and branches of the trees.

The grass was slick with water, and Julia kept her attention centered on the ground, carefully watching each step to keep from slipping. While Julia watched the ground, Tony watched Julia. He had never known that anyone could look so good in jeans and a sweater.

The long strands of her hair were inky black and almost blue in the moonlight, and they curled wildly above Julia's eyes and across her cheeks, spiraling down to hide the classic beauty of her face. But Tony didn't need to see the face to remember its perfection. He had already memorized the changeable hue of Julia's soft gray eyes and the sculpted shape of her shadowed cheekbones that spoke of distant Indian ancestry. He had already tasted the fullness of her lips, lips that beckoned him to steal yet another kiss, a kiss that this time

Tony wouldn't be the one to end. Even her sweet, clean scent haunted him. Julia smelled of fabric softener, cold nights and rain showers, and a sweet, unidentifiable fragrance that clung to her hair, some type of exotic flower that suited her perfectly.

He wanted her.

"How many horses do you have?"

Horses? Tony struggled to pull his mind back where it belonged. "Um . . . I have twelve horses all together, but they aren't all stabled here at the ranch. Some are over at my foreman's place, and four of the wilder ones just spend the winter loose in the pasture. Mostly we only keep work animals around for the ranch, and they're all expected to pull their loads. But last week something caught my eye at the auction, and I decided that this one time I would make an exception. I think you'll agree that I bought something pretty special."

Tony slipped the rusty bolt from its newer silver catch and braced himself against the weight of the barn's enormous red door as it slid sideways on its wheeled track. When the door opened, Tony barely had time to step back before a pair of furry tornadoes rushed out to greet them.

Wild with enthusiasm, the small dogs leaped for Tony's hands and arms, and whined deep in their throats as they tried to lave kisses on any part of him they could reach. Finally, Tony managed to grab both Border collies by their collars just as they made the leap for Julia. The animals fell to the ground in squirming piles of fur, ecstatic at his touch.

"Now *those* dogs don't scare me," Julia assured him. "Something tells me that they don't bite. You can let them go and I'll take my chances."

"No, they won't bite," Tony said, trying to extricate his hand from one of the leather collars while the animal squirmed beneath it, "but they might lick you to death if you're not careful." When he got his hand free and released them, the dogs turned their frantic attentions on Julia and it appeared they were indeed trying to lick her to death, knocking her almost instantly to a seat on the packed ground. Julia's surprised gasp quickly changed to laughter as she put up her hands to ward off their eager tongues. Tony laughed, too, enjoying the sight for a moment before he stepped in to insinuate his body between the animals and Julia. When he reached down to pull Julia to her feet, he didn't let go right away. Instead, he took the opportunity to hold her close. Tony shoved the dogs aside twice with his foot, but the animals immediately returned for more attention, chewing at Tony's heels with almost gentle teeth, and jumping toward Julia with their paws in the air as if they were intent on knocking her down a second time.

"Sit down," Tony ordered, but the collies showed no inclination to listen. Tony shook his head as they rolled on the ground at his feet, paws in the air. Finally Tony told the dogs sternly to go away and this final command they decided to obey. Together, they raced off toward the cattle pens to wake the rest of the animals on the ranch, barking their excitement in strident voices.

"What a pair," Julia said. "If they're supposed to be guard dogs, I think they have a ways to go." She bent down and slapped the dust from her worn blue jeans, her hands tracing a figure that Tony wanted to discover for himself. He turned his head to find something else to concentrate on, but when

Julia said, "Hello there, baby," in a soft, beguiling voice, Tony jerked his head back up to look. Unfortunately he wasn't the one that Julia was speaking to in those sweet tones. She was already inside the barn, moving toward a pair of dark, intelligent eyes that watched them from over the top of the nearest stall.

"That's Kareem," Tony said as Julia stretched out her hand to the animal. It was the first time Tony had been jealous of a horse. "He's been with the ranch a long time and he's a great cattle horse. I think he knows which way a cow is going to break before the animal does herself. In fact, Kareem could probably run a roundup all alone if we gave him a chance."

"Kareem?"

"Yeah, like the basketball star, you know? My son is a longtime basketball fanatic and he insisted on naming the horse. I brought carrots if you want to give him some."

Tony handed Julia the plastic bag he'd filled at the house and she reached in and pulled out a handful. When she closed the plastic bag and stuffed it inside her back pocket, Tony tried not to notice how the denim jeans drew up tight across the back, or how nice they looked that way.

Kareem regally accepted the treat from Julia, his lips reaching out and brushing lightly over her fingers as he took them. The treat disappeared quickly, and when the carrots were gone the horse's ears shifted forward, his soft nicker asking for more. When Julia reached into her pocket to comply, Tony stopped her.

"You'd better save some of those," Tony said.

"You have a lot of friends waiting their turn to see you." Tony flipped a switch on the wall that turned on the long overhead lights and silhouetted three other interested equine faces watching from the line of stalls.

"Oh, Tony! You are so lucky to have all of this."

Yeah, he was. He had everything he'd always wanted, although sometimes he forgot that.

Julia worked her way down the line of waiting horses, obviously enjoying handing out the small carrots and petting velvet-soft noses, while nickers of thanks and whinnies for more treats trailed in her wake. Tony followed behind, smiling at Julia's amusement, as fascinated by the woman as she was by the horses. She shouted with laughter when she turned her back and Tony's big sorrel butted his head against her shoulder in a bid for attention. The horse nearly stole the apple Tony had told her to save for the end, but she managed to step away in time. Finally, Julia had given treats to all the waiting animals and had worked her way to the stall at the very back of the barn, the one Tony had been waiting for.

"Now," Tony said, trying to ignore the pride that spilled out with his words, "come over here and take a look at our new baby."

Julia stepped forward and stood on tiptoe to get a look over the top of the stall door. Tony heard her sharp intake of breath and her envious sigh; it was exactly the way he himself had reacted. "He's absolutely precious," Julia said.

The Arabian colt was lying stretched out in the straw that blanketed his stall and his sleek charcoal-gray coat was almost invisible against the shadows.

At the sound of their voices, the colt raised his head and his small ears pricked forward with interest. Bright, inquisitive eyes turned in their direction.

"He's still so small," Julia said as the colt scrambled to his feet and trotted over to thrust his nose over the gate. His tail was just beginning to grow out and swung in small circles behind him. "He's just a baby."

"Nope, he was already one year old last February, so it's time he started learning what's expected of him. His sire was fifteen hands and he'll probably be about the same, so he'll never be all that big. For a yearling, he's doing just about right."

"Are you going to be doing the training yourself?"

"Not exactly," Tony said. "I'm going to start him out this week, but I'm hoping that eventually my daughter, Angela, will be interested in taking over the training. Actually, I'm hoping she'll be interested at all. The horse is a present for her sixteenth birthday."

"What a lucky girl to get a present like this."

"Yeah. I hope Angela thinks so. I'm sure not going to buy her the car she's been asking for all year. I don't think she's ready to drive, much less own a car, but Angela does, and she's dying to have the freedom her friends seem to have. Maybe this will be enough reason to make her want to stay home."

Tony rarely shared his worries about his daughter. With teenagers people either thought the worst or laughed it off. But instead of offering the normal empty assurances, Julia looked at Tony with sympathy. "It's awfully hard, isn't it?" she asked. "To be able to give children what they want when they don't even know what they want themselves? It must make it difficult to know how to be a good parent."

Her instant understanding was a blessing. She gave no useless advice and said nothing that pigeonholed his daughter with all the other sixteen-year-olds that she had ever met. Her understanding pushed aside all the questions Tony couldn't answer anyway and let him focus on the present. He hoped the colt would bring him closer to his teenage daughter at a time he was afraid they were drifting apart. Julia had known exactly what to say.

Julia reached over top of the gate to pet the colt and he ran his nose along her arm, tickling her with his long whiskers. A gentle smile touched her lips as she glanced up hopefully at Tony. "Can I go inside?" she asked.

The handsome yearling pushed demandingly against her when she stepped through the gate, his long nose bumping her arms as he picked up the sweet smells of the apple and the carrots Julia had been holding. It only took a few seconds before he searched out the treasures, his long nose zeroing in on the treat Julia had been saving especially for him. When Julia presented the apple, the horse plucked the fruit from her hand with one smooth movement and danced away on delicate hooves with the coveted prize held aloft for display. The horse was as graceful as a ballet dancer. Julia had surely never seen a more beautiful animal.

"What's his name?"

"So far he doesn't have one," Tony said. "Angela's birthday isn't until next Friday and I want her to have the pleasure of that decision, so I guess the little fellow will have to be nameless awhile yet."

"Next Friday? That's a long time to keep a thing like this a secret. Certainly she'll notice him in the barn."

"Not my daughter." Tony sighed. "Angela tries hard to stay as far away from the barn and the ranch as possible. The truth is, Angela wasn't very happy when we moved away from the city a few years ago. She was in her second year of middle school and had a circle of friends she ran around with. She didn't want to move and fought against it the whole way. Once we arrived, she didn't really believe that this was where we were going to stay and she's never gotten used to living away from the city. I think pretending like the ranch doesn't really exist is her way of paying me back for taking her out of the world she knew."

Julia felt Tony's pain. Every child should have a parent who cared so much. "How about your son? Does he like living on the ranch?"

Tony's expression softened. "Yeah, he does real well around the ranch; he really loves it. But then my son is a whole lot like me and both of us need to be out in the wide-open spaces to feel at home. We go out on the horses and ride for hours, and it's the city crowds and the traffic and the noise that make us antsy." Tony stood up, stretching his long legs. The colt wandered over and Tony scratched behind his inquisitive, tufted ears, enticing him to lean closer until he rested his entire yearling weight against Tony's legs. He definitely had a way with horses.

They stayed in the stall for hours, playing with

the colt while they talked about children and dreams and life. Relaxing in the stall with Tony was simply the nicest time Julia could remember having in years. She hadn't been kidding when she had told Tony that she usually spent most of her time at work, but it wasn't really because she needed to or even because she wanted to. It was because there was usually nowhere else she would rather be and no one else she would rather be with. On her occasional dates, Julia always found herself watching the clock from beginning to end, forcing herself to make the same small talk, and ticking off the minutes until the evening would be over and she would be free to return home. But tonight with Tony, the minutes and hours flew past as they discussed life and religion and philosophy and almost anything else that they could think of. Julia found that although Tony's views were worldly, his values were not, and often she caught him arguing both sides of an issue until she laughingly conceded to whichever point he was trying to make.

When the apple and carrots were completely gone, the colt grew tired of playing and eventually settled back into his sleep. He lay down in the straw and curled up along Julia's side, warming the leg and hip of that side of her body and reminding her how chilled the rest of her was. The night had aged and early morning had seeped in, bringing with it the coldest hours of the night. Coupled with the moisture in the air, the temperature was almost winter-like and Julia wished she had a horse to keep her other side warm, too. She shivered and ran her hands across her arms to warm away the goosebumps.

"You should have told me that you were cold. We could go inside the house and talk by the fire."

"Let's stay a little longer. I'm not ready to go back inside yet." Julia felt like Cinderella at the ball, enjoying herself, yet knowing reality would come too soon. She wasn't ready for reality yet. "Besides, it's still early."

"Yeah," Tony agreed. "Early in the morning." But his eyes were soft with laughter as he looked down on her seat in the straw. "If you'll give me a minute, I think I can warm you up without us having to go inside."

And after a provocative sentence like that, he walked away. Tony obviously hadn't meant the words the way Julia had taken them. She had thought he was talking about a whole different way to warm up.

When he returned to the stall a few minutes later, Tony had a blue-and-white wool blanket bundled in his arms. "It's been stored in a trunk out here all year. I shook it out as well as I could, but I think it's still going to be a little dusty," he said, opening the gate to the stall. "But it's warm enough to see you through a colder night than this."

"I'm surprised that it gets so cold here. In Phoenix this time of year, it's already sweltering at night. I guess the ground doesn't get a chance to cool off because of all the cement. Even a heavy rainstorm doesn't really help much. It just adds humidity."

He wrapped the woolen blanket around her shoulders, and Julia curled into its warmth, pushing the tickling fringe away from her face. The comfort added by the blanket had been the one thing missing from a perfect evening. Now she could truly say that she'd never been more relaxed. Despite all the fine hotels she had stayed in and all the magnificent convention centers she'd visited, Julia had found the ultimate comfort beneath a scratchy woolen blanket on the straw-covered floor of an old barn.

Tony lifted the edge of the blanket and slid beneath its warmth, his body resting close beside her own. When he slipped his arm around her shoulders, Julia leaned back contentedly into his arms.

"You don't sound like you like living in the city very much," Tony said.

"I keep so busy that I don't really mind it. At first, it was hard to get used to being so boxed in and having my neighbors only an arm's length away. I was raised with lots of space and lots of room to move around, and it was a long walk if I wanted to play with the other kids from school," she said. "For a long time, I thought that was the way it was everywhere. But Phoenix is okay. In fact, I spent three years in Mexico City for college, so I've lived in big cities before."

"When you were growing up, did you live in Mexico or the United States?"

"A little of each place as a teenager, but we spent most of my childhood in Mexico. My father was a fisherman, and in the summertime he took out tourists on the Sea of Cortez. My family lived in a little village perched just above the ocean and the closest city was miles away. During the summer the Americans would pitch tents down the beach and the fishermen would leave their own nets behind and make enough money to last them all year. My parents didn't own very many possessions, but there wasn't much we needed, so we didn't miss it. Rain or shine, my father always brought home dinner so we never went hungry and the one thing we kids had was plenty of freedom. It wasn't until years later, after we visited my cousins in America, that I began to realize how poor we really were."

"Then for you to make it all the way through college and medical school is quite an achievement. You should be proud of yourself."

"It wasn't really all that hard," Julia demurred. "The two college degrees were years apart, and I took advantage of every grant and scholarship I could find on either side of the border. Finally, I discovered American paid scholarships for bilingual students who were willing to commit to four years of work after graduation, and at that point I would have been willing to promise almost anything to get a college education. When I was growing up, no one talked much about going to school, and certainly not college, but I always knew—" Julia stopped. It always made her uncomfortable when she realized she'd been talking only about herself. She shifted uneasily on the straw and drew the blanket higher across her waist, moving her leg a little beneath the weight of the horse. "I didn't mean to bore you with the entire history of my life," she said. "Anyway, everything worked out and here I am."

Tony slipped his hand up to the back of her neck and treated her to a caress that loosened the stiff, tense muscles. Julia leaned back into his touch like a cat seeking affection. "You are not boring me," he said. "You're a very interesting woman." His sweet words warmed her as much as his gentle touch. "So after you went back to school and became a doctor, what made you decide to stay in the United States?"

Julia closed her eyes, sinking into the sensations, enjoying the feel of Tony's hand against her skin. "Because the best equipment and supplies are in the United States and are sometimes difficult to find in Mexico. I try to do what I can to bring the equipment and supplies together with the people that need them the most."

Tony's caress stilled against the back of her neck, his gentle fingers now only lightly brushing her sensitive skin. Julia opened her eyes to find Tony's attention locked on her face, his mouth only inches from her own.

He was going to kiss her. Julia felt she had waited forever for Tony's kiss.

His lips brushed softly across hers with the lightest of pressure, lingering with a teasing touch before withdrawing. But Julia wanted more. She held her breath, hoping, waiting, until Tony's lips again brushed across hers, stopping to press ever so gently, questioning his welcome.

When Julia opened her mouth to him, meeting his tongue with her own, it seemed to answer his question. Julia reveled in the tightening of Tony's arms around her shoulders, and she drank in the feel of his strong hand as he expertly cupped the back of her head, holding her mouth still for his plunder.

And Julia welcomed the plundering.

She released her grip on the rough woolen blanket, leaving it to slip from her arms. Julia had found something that warmed her far better than any blanket. She put her arms up to rest on the muscles of Tony's strong shoulders, and her hands danced across his skin, certain that was where they belonged. She trailed her fingers lightly over the bunched muscles of his forearm and across the longer muscles of his upper arms and shoulders, knowing she had never touched a body more perfectly molded. And Tony's muscles weren't built on a rowing machine at some uptown gym, but were defined by long hours of hard work on the ranch, and the skin of his neck was rough from years spent in the sun, riding the range.

He was exactly as a man should be.

It was amazing how truly soft Julia was. And not just on the outside where Tony could feel the softness of her skin and her hair, but all the way through to the depths of her soul. The childhood poverty, which Julia had experienced and now spoke of so lightly, had only served to make her more compassionate and more concerned with helping to change the world where she could. Funny how the money he'd made had exactly the opposite effect on him.

But Julia was sweet, her actions as well as her looks, and her kisses were pretty darn sweet, too. This woman, who had dropped out of the sky and onto his property, was the woman Tony had somehow missed finding during all of the years he'd been searching. He had been granted a gift, a second chance, and he was old enough to treasure it.

When Julia leaned her head back against the wooden slats of the stall and slipped her arms around his neck, Tony took advantage of the surrender to slant his mouth across hers and deepen the kiss that had become all consuming. Tony wanted Julia like he hadn't wanted a woman in what seemed like decades. His rough fingers tangled in the softness of her hair, brushing curling tendrils from her cheek so he could trail kisses across the soft skin of her face. "You taste so good," he whispered. "Like sun-warmed honey." Julia turned her head to recapture his mouth, and this time she took the responsibility for deepening the kiss almost to the point of no return.

Outside the warm protection of the barn, the heavy storm clouds thickened the night air and let loose with rain and wind that lashed against the solid wooden structure and rattled the glass in the tall casement windows in a violent effort to get inside. But safe from the storm's renewed fury, Tony let his kiss slip from Julia's lips to her forehead to her hair and felt he'd finally achieved something in his life when she sighed and leaned close against his heart, wrapping her arms contentedly around his waist.

For once, Tony had everything he needed to see him through the night.

FOUR

The roar of an engine and sound of a truck door slamming woke him.

"Hey, Ricky. Where's your dad at this morning?"

"I don't know, Ben. He's around here someplace, I guess. By the time I woke up this morning, Dad had already gone outside. I can't believe he actually let us sleep late on a school day for once."

Late? Just how late was it?

"When you find him, will you tell him I'm going to take a run up to Wilcox for supplies? I'll pick up the new harness we ordered while I'm out there and buy the posts for the fence on the upper pasture. I should be back by sometime late this afternoon."

"Okay, I'll let Dad know. Maybe he got a start on the chores this morning. I'll check the barn."

Ricky was coming inside the barn?

Tony slowly eased his stiff shoulder from beneath the dark head of curls that was still pillowed against it and he grimaced as he flexed his fingers to send some blood flowing to the hand and fingers that had fallen asleep. Long, sharp pieces of straw tickled near his ear. Tony brushed it away, and a handful fell from his hair.

Somehow he'd fallen asleep in a stall of his barn,

with Julia in his arms and a colt pressed against their legs, and managed to sleep the whole night through. It was unbelievable. Even more unbelievable was the fact that he and Julia were both still fully dressed. Tony grinned at that one and shook his head. He must really be getting old; he sure wouldn't have slipped up like that in his youth.

He rolled from beneath the woolen blanket and was careful not to disturb the gangly form of the sleeping colt still stretched out near their feet. Julia's head was resting on the straw, and the fingers of one of her hands were tucked beneath her cheek as she slept. She looked as innocent as a child. Tony could have stood there and looked at her forever.

Picking up his abandoned boots by the gate, Tony worked to brush the rest of the clinging straw from his clothes as he slipped from the stall. He managed to get his feet into his boots and made it out to the door of the barn just as Ricky walked around the corner.

"Hi, Dad. You're sure up early."

"Thought I'd come out and give you a hand with feeding the horses this morning and I've just about finished." Tony put his hand on his son's wiry shoulder, turning him away from the barn. "Is your sister out of bed yet?"

Ricky made a face. "Yeah, you know Angela. She's got a mirror set up in the kitchen and stuff lying all over the counter so she can do her hour of makeup and hair while she cooks breakfast."

"If she's cooking breakfast, don't complain. Let's go in and see what's she's making."

The twin smells of pancakes and burnt bacon met them at the kitchen door and Tony thanked heaven for having kids that pitched in with the work. For all the trouble Angela gave him, she still got up and made a hot breakfast for them all, every morning, rain or shine. For that reason alone, Tony knew that his daughter would turn out all right.

"Angela?" There was a big stack of pancakes waiting on a plate on the kitchen table, and there were butter, syrup, and plates set out, but no Angela and no makeup littering the counter. Of course, the bathroom door was closed. When Tony knocked and called her name, the door opened like a shot.

"Okay. So I burnt the bacon. I couldn't help it—I was busy." Always immediately defensive, first thing in the morning until last thing at night.

"I don't care about the bacon. At least there's breakfast on the table," Tony tried.

"I can't do everything by myself in the mornings," his daughter continued, yanking the hot curlers from her normally straight brown hair as she stormed by. For a minute, Tony thought of mentioning all of the chores he and Ricky normally accomplished every day before the boy caught the bus for school. Instead, Tony glanced over Angela's head at the round clock hanging at the end of the dining room. It was already seven o'clock. Time to go.

"You two only have about twenty minutes left before the school bus gets here. You'd better hurry up and finish getting ready if you want to have time to eat."

The next fifteen minutes passed in a rushed blur as the kids found their notebooks and backpacks, which had been summarily abandoned upon their arrival home the previous afternoon.

Breakfast was finally grabbed as they hurried out the door, wrapped in napkins for the walk to the bus stop. Thankfully, neither of his children had yet noticed the airplane sitting out behind the house, but the school bus would pass right by it on the return trip to the highway. Tony would have a lot of explaining to do when they got home.

But in the meantime, he had no complaints about how the morning was working out. Ricky and Angela were gone off to school, Ben had left for Wilcox to do the shopping, and Tony had an entire day stretching ahead of him and a beautiful woman to spend it with.

He ran a mental list of the things that absolutely had to be completed that morning, because what he accomplished that morning was all the work he planned to do for the day. It was the first time since moving back to the ranch that Tony could remember taking the whole afternoon off to play.

Balancing two steaming cups of coffee in his hands, Tony walked across the sun-drenched courtyard between the house and the barn. The grass was still wet with the night's rain, and the reflection of the morning rays on the standing water was nearly blinding to his tired eyes. When he reached the barn, it was a relief to step back inside the cool darkness. A shadow rose from the hay bales on his right, and as his vision cleared, the shadow turned into a blanket-shrouded figure with dark curling hair.

Squinting against the bright sunlight that poured through the doorway, Julia raised one dirty hand to shade her eyes and gifted Tony with her gentle smile. Her hair was wild, a dark halo from which pieces of straw stuck out in every direction, and she had a dark smudge across her cheek and chin. Tony was sure he'd never seen a woman look more appealing.

When Julia abandoned the blanket on the hay bales and stretched like a cat in the morning sun, Tony's mouth went dry. How in the world had he fallen asleep with this woman beside him? Maybe something was wrong with him.

"Would you like some coffee?" He held out the cup, almost afraid to get any closer to her beautiful body, afraid that if she came close enough to touch, he wouldn't be able to keep his hands off her.

"Yes, thanks. Coffee sounds great." She took the cup between her hands and paused to breathe in the aroma. Finally Julia took a sip, closing her eyes before her face disappeared behind the rim of the wide cup. Tony had to look away.

"Is the ground outside still muddy?"

"The ruts on that old runway were already pretty deep," Tony said. Technically it was the truth, but he hadn't actually gone out to check. The subject was one he didn't want to think about yet. The time he had to spend with Julia would end all too soon and she would fly away and out of his life. Of course, Tony knew that she had to return home to her work, but knowing didn't kill the disappointment. "I guess you're probably in a hurry to get back to Phoenix, but since you've waited this long, you'd better delay it at least a few more hours."

Julia reached out her cup-warmed hand and laid it gently on his cheek. "I'd like that. This has been the very nicest of delays."

Tony turned his head to kiss the warm fingers.

"It's hard to believe I'm missing work today. This

is quite a change for me. I'm usually home by Sunday afternoon to get everything ready," she said.

"Except for last night."

"Yes, last night I was late leaving the clinic. And just look where that got me."

They both laughed, but neither one looked away. Finally, Tony broke their connection, sliding his hand over the top of hers, wrapping their fingers together. It felt so right, so natural to take her hand. "If you want to go in the house and get cleaned up, I'll get the animals fed out here. Then maybe we can talk about what you would like to do today."

"What are my choices?"

Tony didn't mention what *his* choices would have been. "It's a surprise. You'll have to wait and see," he said, giving her a little swat on her slender hip as he brushed past. "The kids have already left for school, so the house is all yours. Go ahead and shower and whatever else it is you women do. If you can't find what you need, check Angela's bathroom; she has two of everything."

The promise of a hot shower sounded too wonderful to pass up. Inside the house, Julia found the front bathroom easily enough, but the supplies she unearthed were Spartan, the bathroom shelves holding only a manly assortment of deodorant and aftershave, and a type of generic shampoo Julia wouldn't have dreamed of using on her hair. She just hoped that when she found Angela's bathroom, it would come with a better selection.

The first door in the hallway that Julia opened obviously belonged not to Tony's daughter, but to his teenage son. The walls of the bedroom were covered with giant color posters of basketball players and rodeo stars, and the carpeting was littered with the boy's dirty clothes. Julia laughed and closed the door. It was good to see that at least one room in Tony's house wasn't kept spotless. It made her feel more at home.

On her second door, Julia knew she had found the room she was looking for.

Angela's bedroom was all girl, decorated in lace and pastels, and the floor was covered in thick white carpeting. The small room was almost overwhelmed by an enormous canopied bed that rested against the far wall, complete with a white canopy cover tied with rose-edged ribbons. Beyond the bed, the door to a pink-and-white bathroom was partially open.

While Tony's son had favored posters of basketball players and broncobusters to decorate his room, Tony's daughter had shied away from sports figures and instead had covered every inch of available space with posters of movie stars. Or one movie star, rather.

With her long, platinum hair hanging to her hips and her ripe, hourglass figure, even Julia would be hard put not to recognize the famous Marta Marquez, the starlet who had once sent Cimmerron Pictures rocketing to the top of the competition. Marta Marquez had used her work as a cover model to become the pinup girl of the previous decade, and her image had been everywhere. When she signed the contract with Cimmerron, she had assured that the fledgling film company would become a success.

Moving beyond movie stardom, Marta Marquez

had eventually claimed icon status and a whole generation of girls had spent their teenage years trying to mimic Marta's wild clothing and pouting looks, but now, years later, she had faded from the scene. Julia thought she was still putting out movies, and she'd seen the woman's face in a commercial or two, but Marta Marquez certainly wasn't the star she once had been. Except that Angela was obviously still a big fan, and the proof covered the walls.

On Angela's bathroom door, the largest of the many posters displayed Marta Marquez's famous figure from head to toe, with very little material placed in between, and along one long, bare leg, in black ink, was scrawled "To Angela, with all my love."

So Tony's daughter had actually met the actress. No wonder the girl was starstruck.

Pushing the bathroom door open the rest of the way, Julia stepped inside and turned on the light over the mirror. The pink-and-white bathroom was a girl's dream with both a tub and shower and a long countertop beneath the shelves. And when Tony said that Angela had two of everything, he hadn't been kidding after all. Julia smiled. Tony had sounded disgusted, but his daughter's obsession didn't seem like such a bad thing to her.

An array of makeup not to be rivaled in a big-city department store was crowded beside the rose-tiled sink, and from the oak shelves above the sink hung wires that led Julia to curling irons, blow dryers and every other beauty appliance ever designed to be plugged into the wall. Inside the roomy shower, Julia found shampoo and conditioner with the logo of a famous Beverly Hills salon and almost shouted as she held up the prize; she would never have dreamed of buying such an expensive brand of shampoo for herself, but it would be wonderful to try it out. Julia might have to put on the same wrinkled clothes after she took her shower, but she would be washing her hair in style.

The sting of the hot water melted away the remaining stiffness of the night from Julia's body. Actually, she'd slept surprisingly well, considering she had been inside a strange barn, in the scratchy straw, with a wiggly colt for a companion. She'd slept in the stable a lot as a child, and waking to the familiar smells had been like being there again, young and carefree. Julia had awakened from her dreams with a smile. Of course, when she was a child their family's stable had been nothing so grand, nothing more than four walls and a roof. And Julia had never slept in the arms of a man too sexy for words. No doubt *that* was why she'd had such wonderful dreams.

After she had finished showering and dressing, Julia exchanged the expensive shampoo and conditioner for a blow dryer and diffuser and took the time to tame her wild hair with the round brush. Julia ignored the fact that she was usually ready to leave for work in half the time she was taking to get ready today. For the first time since Julia had met Tony, she wouldn't look like she was either a drowned rat or a creature that had emerged from the straw. Julia couldn't help but wonder if Tony would like the results.

She smoothed lotion over her face and secured her hair back with a clip before using her own meager selection of cosmetics from her purse. When Julia returned to the living room, Tony was already inside. His low whistle was all the reward Julia had hoped for.

"Honey, I swear you get prettier every time I see you."

Julia could have said the same about him. Standing in the living room, framed by a sharp ray of morning sunlight that splayed through the picture window, Tony was so handsome that it nearly took Julia's breath away. He had changed into blue jeans and a faded work shirt the color of the afternoon sky. His newly shaven cheeks flashed a dimple when he smiled.

"I'll bet you say that to all the women who show up at your front door." Julia tried to look away from his smile, but it was difficult.

"Maybe," he qualified, "but since you're the only one I've ever invited to come inside, I can't say for sure." The look on Tony's face made Julia suddenly very thankful for the storm that had nearly killed her.

"So what did you decide we're going to do today?" she asked. Personally, Julia was happy just staring at him, but she didn't think he would want to stand there all day just for that.

"Well, If you like the idea, I thought we could pack up some food and go on a picnic. We'll take a couple of horses and spend the whole day up high in the mountains."

It was exactly what she would have chosen herself—a day in the middle of nowhere, far from the hurry of the real world. "A picnic sounds great, but I can't drag you away from your ranch for the whole day. I'm sure you have other things you have to get done."

That warm smile returned beneath his dark mustache and Julia's toes curled inside her tennis shoes when Tony said, "I can't think of a thing I need to do today that's more important than getting to know you better."

She would have gone anywhere with him after a statement like that. When Julia told him so, Tony winked at her. "Good," he said. "Then let's get going. If we leave now, we'll make it in time for lunch."

An old, dented blue pickup truck had been pulled around the front of the house and parked in the driveway by the wall. A two-horse trailer was attached behind, and a pair of long, silky tails hung over the trailer gate. Julia glanced in the trailer at the waiting animals. "When you said we would take horses, I thought we'd be riding them, not taking them for a drive in the country."

Tony laughed. "We're only going to be driving part of the way. If we start the ride down here, it will take hours, so I thought we'd start a little higher up in the hills where it's cooler. I know of a real pretty area where we can stop for lunch and eat beside a waterfall."

He turned the truck out of the driveway and they bounced through the desert on a dirt track far too rough to be termed a road. In the side mirror, Julia kept an anxious eye on the horse trailer, certain it was going to overturn at any second and drag them down with it. Around them, the scrub-covered soft desert slopes of the hills moved into the high-country, tree-lined majesty of the towering mountains. The last of the winter snow tipped the tops of the peaks that soared above the desert floor, standing fierce, beautiful and awesome.

"Do you drive up here very often?" Julia braced

her hands against the roof and the dashboard as Tony eased the truck over another huge boulder that blocked their way. She was sure that no one would drive this road any more than necessary.

"We have to come up to the high pasture at least twice each year for the cattle roundups," Tony said. He gunned the engine up the gravelly incline. "It used to be that you couldn't even get a vehicle up here," he said, obviously proud of the gully they were driving in. "We used to have to load up everything we needed on mules or horses and pack it in, walking the animals and wasting an entire day to get there. It was hard work to make that trip. A walk like that could make even a hardened cowboy sore."

Julia banged her elbow hard on the doorframe as the truck slid sideways in the dirt before its tires regained traction. She wasn't sure that driving the road in the truck was any great improvement over Tony's "old days." She was going to be as sore as any hardened cowboy.

At the end of the rough, thirty-minute ride up the hillside, Tony pulled the truck to a stop in the shade of a graceful old mesquite tree and reached down to set the emergency brake. Although beautiful and shady, the spot he had chosen was little different than a hundred other such spots they had driven past along the way. Julia didn't see any reason to stop. She certainly didn't see a waterfall.

"Here we are," Tony said.

"*Where* are we?" Julia asked, climbing out of the cab and stretching the tense muscles in her legs.

Tony grinned at her disparaging tone. "At the entrance to paradise," he assured her.

He opened the trailer gate and easily backed the

horses down the ramp with practiced movements.
The animals waited patiently for him at the bottom of the ramp, rubbing their heads against the
metal corner of the trailer. Tony was beside the
truck, filling the leather saddlebags with the pack-
ages he had brought, and he worked swiftly with
practiced and confident movements, wasting little
effort. Julia took pleasure in watching him. Tony
knew the horses and the tack and everything there
was to know about the land they stood on. He
would be at home working on the ranch, at home
with only a horse and saddle on thousands of
empty acres.

To Julia's eyes, Tony represented the epitome of
a true cowboy, a man completely at ease in his envi-
ronment, a man who took nothing for granted. He
was the one who all the cowboy songs were about,
the one who walked off into the sunset at the end
of the movie. When Tony finished with the loading
and walked toward Julia in the dappled sunlight,
with his dark hat set low over his forehead and the
leather saddlebags tossed over his wide, strong
shoulders, Julia was certain she had never seen a
more beautiful man.

"You should be in the movies," she said, speaking
her thoughts aloud. *"The Last Cowboy,* or something."

Well," Tony said, "I suppose I should take that as
a compliment, but I think I'll just pass on the
whole movie thing if you don't mind. There's already plenty of folks out there who want to be
movie stars, but I'm happy right where I am." Un-
tying the horses from the trailer gate, Tony
handed Julia the reins to a handsome bay mare
with white stockings and soft brown eyes. He led

the way down the faint path with his sorrel, the tall grass and brush springing back into place behind the animal's long red tail. Julia followed with her own horse, trying to keep the sorrel's red tail in sight.

There were no trees growing, except for those along the road, and the rocky sand of the path they walked on supported little growth besides thick grasses that sent tall stalks higher than Julia's head. The path led slightly downhill and soon the tall grasses became so thick that Julia had to hang back a few feet to avoid the pieces that sprang into place after the sorrel's passage. It wasn't long until she was following the sound of the horse instead of the horse itself.

And the lowland path was miserable. Flies droned through the grasses, grasshoppers leaped out from underfoot, and gnats whined around Julia's face in bothersome circles no matter how many thousands of times she shoed them away. When at last the land began to rise sharply, promising higher ground just ahead, Julia hurried forward, anxious to catch up to Tony and leave the weeds and bugs behind. She stepped over the top of the incline with huge relief—and stumbled right into a shallow creek beyond.

"Watch your step," Tony called from somewhere upon the bank. "There's a creek down there."

"Thanks a whole lot," Julia mumbled. The day was hot, but the water was cold and Julia's sense of humor almost deserted her at the instant cooling. When she stood up in the stream, she was completely wet from the waist down. Julia waded out of the creek to trade the weight of the water that streamed from her jeans for that of the mud that quickly coated her tennis shoes.

Somewhere it must be written that Julia would always be wet and muddy around Tony.

Julia's horse waited patiently for her at the crest of the hill, interestedly watching her progress until she reached the hill and retrieved the hanging reins. "I suppose you knew that the creek was here, too," Julia scolded the mare. The bay tossed her head impatiently, obviously pointing out which one of them was still on dry land. "Someone could have told me," Julia muttered to herself. "Now, even the horse is laughing at me."

Julia squished her way up the muddy bank in her wet, slippery shoes until she again reached the narrow path. This time, she took a sharp right at the top of the hill and found that the path turned into the beginning of the road she should have stayed on all along. A few yards farther, where the dirt road widened, she saw Tony, already mounted and waiting for her. From his vantage point on the horse, Julia was sure he had seen the entire thing. Julia couldn't actually see Tony's grin beneath the shadow of his black Stetson, but she had no doubt it was there. She had to admit that he was doing better than she would have been. If it had been Tony who had fallen in the stream, she would have been laughing like crazy.

"Do you need me to hold the mare still for you while you mount up?"

His question was polite and he showed no sign of a smile, but as Julia put her foot in the stirrup and swung easily up onto the horse's back, she hoped the look she sent Tony was disdainful enough.

After making a fool of herself by falling into the creek, it was a relief to be able to do at least something right.

"I take it that's a no," Tony said dryly. "Obviously you've ridden before. Did you have horses to ride in your little town in Mexico?"

With a slight pressure of her knees, Julia urged the mare forward. "Yep. When I was growing up, nearly everyone in the village owned a horse. Even if you only had a shack to live in, you still had a horse or two out in the corral and we rode almost every day. It was just the way it was."

"I'm glad to hear it," Tony said. "Then, since you've had so many hours in the saddle, we'll go the fun way to the waterfall and see just how good you are."

"Actually, I said I'd spent a lot of time on horseback," Julia corrected. "My family never did get around to buying a saddle."

Tony's laugh rang out, spooking his horse into a sideways dance. Then Tony urged the horse forward into a slow trot and Julia's mount followed suit.

The high desert they rode through was pristine and empty, except for the white faces of cattle that watched suspiciously from thickets or lumbered away at the sound of the horses' approach. The scraggly brush and tall grasses that grew where Tony had parked the truck gave way to majestic yuccas that reached their sharply pointed swords toward the sky like avenging warriors, and dark red ironwood bushes whose twisted limbs could be seen in expensive furniture popular throughout the desert southwest. Enormous boulders littered the landscape, as if set down by a long-ago giant, and a wide stream wound back and forth across their path, whispering as it tumbled alongside and providing a musical backdrop to the awesome scenery.

"I could stay riding out here forever," Julia said, and she meant exactly that. The wild landscape, the freedom, the familiar feeling of a horse's steady gait beneath her had been such a big part of her life, and it felt so right to have them back. "It's been such a long time," she said. "I hadn't realized that I missed riding so much."

A mile or so later, the rolling hills that had greeted them came to an end and the almost-barren landscape leveled out into a high plateau, a ridge set far above the world with only the soaring mountains for a backdrop. A lone hawk circled the rugged ridge and his lonely hunting call was swallowed up in the unending emptiness as his fleeting shadow dusted the ground at Julia's feet. She turned the horse to follow the vision of the hawk's dance until the bird became no more than a distant speck in the sky. By the time Julia returned her attention to the earth and the ride, she'd fallen far behind Tony.

She grinned and urged her mare into a quick canter across the hard-packed plain, leaning low over the saddle and gathering handfuls of the horse's long mane. Now was her chance to have some fun; Tony had said that he wanted to race.

The mare was a runner, stretching out in enjoyment as she gathered speed, and Julia stretched with her, crouching low over her withers to defeat the push of the wind, encouraging the horse to lengthen her stride and to eat up the rapidly disappearing distance between her and Tony. The heavy sand on the path they rode muffled the telling sound of the rapid fire of the mare's hooves, and Julia was able to reach a point only a few yards behind him before Tony finally looked back and saw her. She said nothing, but waited until she was well past him to call out the challenge. "I'll race you to that big palo verde by the rocks."

There was no doubting which tree Julia meant: the blue-green giant shone almost Day-Glo in the bright afternoon sun. Julia didn't wait for Tony's answer before urging her horse faster; he didn't seem the type to walk away from a contest and she wanted all the advantage she could get.

Julia was almost halfway to the tree and was beginning to think she had a real chance of winning the race when she heard the rhythmic thrum of his horse's hooves coming up behind her and Tony's goading laughter drawing closer. He had caught up with her faster than Julia had dreamed possible and he was already only a few feet behind. It was obvious that he would easily catch up and pass her before the end of the race. Julia shot a quick glance behind her, mentally measuring the decreasing distance between them. She'd meant to spare only a single glance over her shoulder, but the image of Tony riding hard behind her was one from which Julia could not bring herself to look away.

Tony was serious about the race and only the slightest hint of a grin showed that he already knew he was going to win. He controlled his horse easily and rode as though he and the horse were really one creature. Tony was obviously a man born in the saddle, born to run a ranch in the desert, and born to take a living from a hard, unforgiving Arizona landscape. He looked wild and gorgeous with his dark hair flying back from his face. He was primitive and powerful, holding tight control over his thousand-pound animal . . . and he was sexy as anything she had ever seen. Julia could feel the intensity of the concentration he centered on the race, and she dreamed of having that same intensity focused on her alone. She wanted that formidable concentration and she wanted Tony's undivided attention. She wanted his arms of corded muscle to close tightly around her and hold her close. She wanted those kisses that enthralled her, kisses that became deeper, more consuming, and completely unstoppable until—

"Julia! Look out!"

Julia didn't see the huge jackrabbit until after it had already shot beneath the hooves of her mare and was bounding away into the brush at the side of the trail. By then it was already too late.

"Whoa!" The wild ride began and Julia was swung around and around, up and down, as her gentle mare transformed herself into a bucking bronco. Julia heard Tony's anxious shout, but the words of his instructions were muffled and lost in the twirling blur of color and sound. There was no calming the animal, no regaining control, only seeing the rodeo ride through until the mare calmed on her own, or somehow getting off of the animal without killing herself. Julia managed to hold on through three more bone-jarring twists before she decided that she hadn't missed this part of riding and that she'd had enough. She was waiting for the right moment, the right opportunity, measuring the rhythm of the ride with a familiarity that came back as easily as riding a bicycle. The trick was not to stay on the horse—it was to get off safely.

When the mare momentarily stopped her wild spin and reared up on her back legs, pawing the air like the Lone Ranger's horse, Silver, Julia was at last given her chance. Without hesitation, she took it. Before the mare could get all four hooves back on the ground to begin the cycle again, Julia made her leap, using all of her strength to push away from the saddle, away from the dangerous, sharp hooves. Relieved of her onerous burden, the mare trumpeted her victory and raced off across the never-ending plateau. Julia crashed to the ground on her knees and the palms of her hands, but she barely noticed the pain. It had been a long time since she'd had to jump off a bucking horse and she considered herself darned lucky that she hadn't broken her neck.

"Julia!" Tony leaped off of his horse, threw the reins to the ground, and was at her side in seconds. "Are you all right? Are you hurt? I'm so sorry. I've never seen that mare do anything like this."

Julia looked up at him from her seat in the dirt and smiled at his distress. Gingerly, she brushed the packed dirt from the small scrapes on her hands, glancing at her palms to make sure there was no real damage. "Sure, I'm fine." Then Julia realized that the mare was gone, out of sight across the empty landscape. "I'm sorry about losing your horse, though. I should have tried to hold on to her."

"Should have tried to hold on to her?" Tony picked up his reins and tossed the end over a low mesquite tree, tethering his own horse. "Forget about the mare, and anyway, she'll come back after she calms down a bit or she'll find her way back to the ranch. I'm just glad you weren't hurt badly when you were thrown. Hell, Julia, I was so worried when I saw you fly off."

"I *wasn't* thrown," Julia said adamantly. She was almost insulted that Tony had suggested it. "I've never been thrown by a horse in my life. I jumped off before she could throw me off."

His expression lightened to almost a smile. "Let me see your hands," he said. Tony crouched down beside her on the dirty ground and gently took Julia's hands in his. Studying the small scratches that crossed her palms, he finished brushing away the rocks and dirt.

"I'm really fine," Julia repeated.

The dirt and rocks were all gone, but still he didn't release her. When Tony lifted her palm to his mouth and pressed his lips against the small abrasions there, Julia forgot all about any remaining pain. Now she really was fine, better even than she'd been before the fall, and with a few more kisses from Tony, she would be completely wonderful. He rose to his feet in one smooth motion and used Julia's captured wrists to pull her up with him—and directly into his arms. "What you are, Julia Huerta, is one damned amazing woman and I am so lucky that you dropped into my life."

His arms slipped from entangling Julia's hands to wrap firmly around her waist, and she leaned willingly into the embrace. Truthfully, the chance to touch Tony again, to feel his strength and his kisses, seemed well worth the few small scratches she had sustained in the fall. There was no need for bandages or balm to ease the scrapes; Julia's palms rested painlessly against the worn-soft cotton of Tony's blue shirt, and the feel of his body against her own was all the medicine she would ever need.

His hands drifted lightly up from Julia's waist to her shoulders and back down over her back, brushing the encrusted dirt from her shirt and then from the seat of her jeans, where his hands momentarily stilled. The dirt on her still-damp jeans was thickly caked, but Tony seemed to have lost all interest in brushing it off; his hands just rested there, holding her against him, burning through the material. Julia's heart was racing, but it was no longer from the adrenaline of the ride. When she finally remembered to breathe, she had to gasp to fill her deprived lungs with air. She raised her gaze to Tony's darkly handsome face, feeling the heat and the desire that she shared, waiting for the kiss she prayed would follow and anxious to have so much more.

And Tony didn't disappoint her. Pulling her body tighter against his, Tony kissed her with his entire self, trapping Julia with the strength of his arms, holding her prisoner as he claimed her lips with his own. She welcomed the press of him and the heat of him. The evidence of his desire pressing intimately against her told her that Tony felt just as she did, that he wanted everything she did. The attraction that had simmered between them since their first meeting had built into an unstoppable fire that burned her with the need to get closer. And she wanted to be burned.

Julia moaned breathlessly, drinking in the sensations as Tony traced his knowing lips across her cheek. His lips claimed her, branded her, lightly touched her mouth and brushed softly against her closed eyelids before climbing to rest for a moment against her hair. Then Julia felt his hot breath on the back of her neck.

On the back of her neck?

"Hey, cut it out!" Squirming out of Tony's tight embrace, Julia turned around and pushed away the equine nose that was nuzzling the back of her hair. She rubbed her hand over the tickle on her neck.

"See? I told you she would come back when she calmed down," Tony said. He picked up the reins that trailed in the dirt behind the mare, and led the horse over to be tied beside his own mount at the mesquite tree.

"I'm glad she came back. I guess my hair smells good enough to eat," Julia said, refastening the hair clip that the horse had managed to work loose.

"I'm willing to bet that every inch of you does."

Julia's gaze snapped to his. He stood a few feet away and didn't touch her, but the air between them nearly flickered with electricity. The tension was back, and Julia was ready and willing to take full advantage of it no matter what tomorrow might bring. But the horse's interruption had evidently restored Tony's common sense, because he quickly looked away from her and broke the connection. Keeping his eyes on the task, he crossed to the loaded saddlebags and began rummaging inside. When he started pulling out the food they'd packed for their lunch, Julia also turned away.

Although disappointed, she was glad the decision had been taken from her. She wanted Tony more than she'd ever wanted anything in her life, but the time had to be right for both of them, and obviously the time was not right for Tony. The best things in life weren't free; Julia's mother had at least been correct about that.

So, instead of jumping Tony's bones in the nearest shade as she wanted to do, Julia headed across the trail toward the creek and concentrated on how refreshing that water was going to feel against her heated skin. Julia stumbled twice while going down the low bank; her knees were weak.

FIVE

The warm afternoon breeze whispered of approaching summer as it slipped through the tall desert grasses and sent ripples rushing across the shallow stream. The remains of their abandoned lunch rested within the shady roots of an old cottonwood tree a few feet away, and while Tony checked on the horses, Julia stretched out alongside the stream. Her shoes were left beside the lunch and she pushed her bare toes deeply into the warm sand and enjoyed the slide of the sand as it brushed across her skin. She rested on her elbows, watching the water until the shimmers of sunshine became too much, then leaned back in the sand and closed her eyes, drinking in the warmth of the sun against her face. Out of the whole world, this was exactly where she wanted to be.

With her eyes closed, Julia concentrated on the sound of the water as it rushed over the rocks that stood in its way, and she listened to the buzz of the lazy flies circling in the tall grasses. The sun and clouds danced patterns across her eyelids, sending her into a dreamlike state until she heard Tony's footsteps and a shadow crossed the sunny patterns and sent them scurrying away. "What a wonderful day this has been," she said, although Julia knew that whatever way she expressed it, it would still be an understatement. "It sure beats any day I would have spent at the office."

"Oh, I don't know," Tony said, his voice a deep, sexy drawl. "I think playing doctor with you sounds pretty good. You can give me a check-up anytime you want."

The words made her mouth go dry. Then Julia heard the splash as Tony stepped into the water. When his shadow passed over her again, Julia opened her eyes to a picture she was sure she would never forget.

Tony had taken off his boots and waded into the small stream, standing ankle-deep while the drops of water dampened his blue jeans all the way to his knees. The afternoon breeze that cooled the day danced across the loose windblown strands of Tony's dark hair, adding a perfect frame to his laughing dark eyes. His smile was intimate, meant for her alone, and Julia found it impossible to look away as he crossed the creek to stand in front of her.

When he stopped, only inches away, the smile in Tony's eyes changed, growing promising, intent, and smoldering. His look caressed Julia like a whispered touch and sent her blood singing through her veins. Julia sat up on the bank, yearning to touch him, reaching toward Tony with her body as well as her hands, wanting him closer. Her lips already tingled in anticipation of his kiss and her breathing was shallow and fast despite the fact that Tony had yet to even touch her.

And she wanted Tony to touch her, prayed that

this would be the moment, because staying away from him was impossible.

In the short eternity since they had met, Tony had gone from stranger to almost lover and all of Julia's being had become focused on that final step of consummation. The constant proximity to him was keeping Julia on the sharp edge of desire, as every hour she discovered more reasons she wanted Tony and more things she wanted him for. She felt as close to him as though they had known each other for years, as though they had always been a part of each other's lives, and all Julia could think was how much closer she wanted to get.

She reached out to draw him the last few feet to her side, touching her hand to his, and her single motion brought the desired effect. Tony kept Julia's hand entwined in his own as he moved out of the water and up the bank to kneel at her side. He never broke the connection of their gazes as he lowered himself to his knees and their bodies barely touched in the sand. One of his knees was planted close beside her hip, and the pressure was only a tease; it wasn't nearly enough. Julia slipped her hand free of his and put her fingers gently against the inside of that knee, until Tony eased his weight off of it and allowed Julia to guide it to the other side of her body. Now Tony straddled her in the sand, and when Julia looked up into his eyes, she knew that this time he would not turn away and there would be no going back. The die was cast and she had never been so sure of her reward.

With gentle pressure, Tony pushed her back until Julia was again lying against the warm sand

and she was cushioned both above and below. Then he sat back slowly, resting his weight against his heels. Very, very slowly. And with each inch that Tony moved, the pressure of his body against hers became more intimate, more demanding, until his blatant desire was as clear to her as her own and only the constriction of their clothing kept them apart. But it still wasn't enough; Julia wanted Tony closer yet. She wanted to feel skin against skin, his against hers. She ran her hands restlessly across Tony's shoulders and over his chest. She pulled the tail of his shirt from his jeans and slid her hands into the slight bend of the denim.

Tony shuddered at her touch. He ended the game abruptly by taking both of Julia's hands from where they would have wandered, and held both wrists to pin them to the ground above her. Now, she was his prisoner.

"You're going way too fast, lady," he whispered. "And I want time to play."

His kisses, though, were anything but playful. The sweet touch of his lips began at a point just behind her left ear, delivering slow, teasing kisses that scalded the skin of her neck, her cheek, her jawline, everywhere but her aching lips that longed for his touch. His kisses forged a burning trail across the rise of Julia's collarbone and finally settled to whisper sweet, shivery words into her ear, avoiding her lips altogether. And his hands, oh, his hands never stopped moving.

Tony had quickly breached the slim protection of her shirt and sweater, sliding a warm palm up across the sensitive skin of her stomach, until his fingertips fluttered like the touch of a butterfly along the line of her ribs. When the knowing heat of his palm finally reached her breasts, touching and brushing over and over, first one and then the other, Julia twisted beneath him. She was frantic to free her own hands from their imprisonment, frantic to take the teasing love-play further, frantic to beg Tony never to stop.

"Not just yet, darling, not yet," he whispered, his breath a shivery fire against her skin. Tony's fingertips circled a sensitive nipple, then captured it and squeezed gently, sending Julia's body into an upward spiral that climbed to the heavens and left her shaking with need. Julia gasped for breath as she returned to earth. She'd had enough games and had waited too long already. She wanted Tony, wanted to claim him, and wanted him to claim her. And she wanted it now.

With the knowledge of Eve, Julia looked into the slow burn of Tony's gaze. "I've heard it can be very dangerous for a man to walk around"—she shifted her hips—"like that. You really should do something about it."

She felt the muscles of his shoulders tighten. His thumb brushed over her breast and she gasped. A smile started deep inside Tony's dark gaze and rose to grace his lips. "I would never argue with the doctor," he said. It was almost a whisper. Tony lowered his head, capturing a swollen nipple through the material of Julia's shirt, and leaving the round wet print of his mouth on her pink sweater. When Julia moaned softly, mindless once more, Tony pushed the confining sweater and shirt up and out of the way, applying the pulling heat of his mouth again with only the thin lace of Julia's meager bra to separate them. When Tony lifted his head to look into her eyes, Julia was terribly afraid that he was going to stop.

But he didn't stop. Instead, Tony reclaimed her lips with his own, finally giving her the kiss she wanted and needed and was ready to beg him for. He released the hands he had taken prisoner and at last Julia was free to explore Tony's sculpted body in return. To touch. To hold. To savor.

Julia reveled in the feel of the solid weight above her, pressing her down. He felt so right there, his body against hers, and his knowing touch and deep, rich kisses sent the world spinning around her. Julia shoved aside the restrictive material of his shirt that lay between them, sliding her hands down into the waistband of his jeans, and then into the line of thin elastic she found just inside. Her fingers crept forward, tracing the elastic line, settling in the warmth, and working their way toward the buttons that Julia couldn't see but still held as her goal. She had almost reached them when Tony's sharp intake of breath abruptly ended their kiss.

"Julia." Her name was like poetry on his lips, the single word stirring her, making her ache for their shared fulfillment. "Are you sure this—today, here—is what you want?"

Even now he was putting her desires above his own. It was the ultimate aphrodisiac.

"I'm very sure. I want you now, Tony."

Her words created a firestorm. His shirt was off in a flash of blue, and he spread it out over the sand, the material creating a place that was nearly large enough for her entire body. Tony slid his hands beneath her knees and shoulders, easily lifting her into his arms and setting her back down in exactly the place he wanted her. Then her sweater and shirt, too, were gone, pulled over her head in a single movement and tossed aside before Julia could even try to help. The bra didn't last a second.

Tony's kiss followed Julia down, enticing her to dance with him directly into the flames. She slipped easily into the all-consuming desire. His tongue mated with hers in imitation of the act she so wanted and when Tony's hot mouth returned to her breast, Julia was certain she had died and gone to heaven.

Except that heaven wasn't complete, because she still couldn't *really* touch him. There was time for only truly important words. "You need to take off *all* your clothes," she whispered.

To Julia's delight he obeyed her request and eased away from her to stand up and to slide his jeans over his slim hips. Against his underwear, the outline of his desire was enough to make Julia start removing the rest of her own clothes. Then Tony's hands settled over her own.

"Let me."

It seemed to take him forever to undo only one button, or maybe it was that time had decided to stand still. As he worked the zipper loose, Tony's rough knuckles repeatedly grazed the skin of Julia's stomach and he used the opportunity to slide his hands almost everywhere on her body. At last the zipper came down, one small tug at a time, and with each tug, Tony caressed her exposed skin so thoroughly that Julia's breathing was ragged and she started again to try to pull off the pants by herself.

"Don't be in such a hurry, honey. I'll take care of

you." His words were muffled as his lips moved across the skin above her hipbone. His mustache teased the skin his lips had warmed.

At long last Tony finally began to remove her confining jeans—one leg at a time, one inch at a time—and each inch of skin he uncovered was treated to the same, thorough touch, the same, thorough tasting, until Julia was mindless with his sweet torture. Then, finally, only Julia's small scrap of white underwear remained.

"You're even more beautiful than I had dreamed," Tony said. "And I have been dreaming of this since the first moment I saw you standing in the rain." He slid one finger slightly beneath the elastic leg band of the simple white triangle of material. Julia felt the world spin and was unable to stop herself from pressing against the palm of his hand, even as she reached up to pull him down to her.

"Wait," he whispered.

The warmth of the sun above and sand below were nothing compared to the heat of Tony's knowing hand with its gentle touch. Small, slow circles from his fingers set Julia gasping, wanting, aching. Then the circles changed and his hand danced a rhythm that plucked and pulled, playing her as sweetly as he had played the guitar the night before. When Tony's mouth finally lowered again to her breast, sucking the taut nipple into its heat, Julia shattered, explosions of color washing over her.

"Now," she said. "Please, now."

Tony reached over to where his jeans lay, crumpled in a heap, and took a small foil package out of one of the pockets. He was very glad he had planned ahead for this moment—at the risk of offending Julia—but right now she looked anything but offended. He quickly shed his underwear, and carefully put the condom on.

When at last Tony's weight settled again where Julia wished him to be—this time without the restriction of clothing between them—and he pushed deep inside of her, the fullness and sweetness were everything Julia had ever dreamed of and more.

It was paradise.

SIX

The late afternoon sun had dipped low on the horizon by the time Julia rode the mare over the top of the last hill and saw Tony's pickup truck waiting for them in the distance. The ride had been long, she had been baked by the hot sun, and there was a pound of scratchy sand inside her pants; the day had passed far too quickly.

Working easily together, it took Tony and Julia almost no time to unload the nearly empty saddlebags and coax the horses into the trailer for the short drive home. Tony said little as they worked, but smiled often, and every accidental brush of his hand was a pleasure Julia looked forward to. She would have labored alongside him all day for no more payment than that.

In almost no time, they were jouncing along in the pickup truck on the road to the ranch. This time, Julia knew to keep her hands and feet braced against the metal cab to keep from being knocked unconscious, and she listened as Tony told funny stories about his life on the ranch. His slow, quiet way of talking made his tales all the more humorous, and though Julia had little to add, she was happy just to sit quietly and drink it all in. Who could have guessed that besides being caring and kind, Tony would be funny and entertaining as well? He was the man every woman dreamed of finding. Julia felt as though she had accidentally stumbled into the one thing that she'd always wanted.

It wasn't until Tony turned off of the long bumpy road and pulled the truck to a stop in the ranch's circular driveway that reality finally intruded into Julia's day; she had been trying hard to pretend reality didn't exist. "It's already getting pretty late," Tony said, when she started to help him unload the horses. "I'll take care of things out here and you'd better go see if that runway ever dried out."

Without waiting for an answer, he went immediately back to work, letting the trailer gate drop open with a loud crash that spooked both the horses inside. Julia's spirits crashed with it. There was nothing for her to do that would help him and it suddenly seemed that there was little else for either of them to say. Worse, Tony didn't even glance in her direction as he backed the first horse down the trailer ramp. The dried mud crunched beneath the horse's feet as he led it across the driveway to the barn.

And Julia stood there and watched him walk away.

It was late on a day that Julia had hoped would never end. Now it seemed abruptly over.

As she made the walk along the long fence to the field where her airplane had waited all night, a part of Julia hoped the confining mud would still be there, thick and heavy, holding the airplane and forcing her to stay a little longer. Even a few more hours to spend in Tony's company would be reason enough. But nature appeared to be finished hand-

ing out favors to Julia. The pocketed runway that
had nearly been a stream the night before had
dried in the sun to white-gray squares that cracked
sharply at her step and crumbled away beneath the
soles of her tennis shoes. The vibration of the airplane alone would be enough to shake it free. She
could no longer find any excuse to stay.

Julia walked slowly on her return trip to Tony's
house as she tried to commit to memory the pieces
of his world. She whispered good-bye as she passed
the long, low wall and breathed in the scent of the
fragrant honeysuckle that clung to the wooden gate.
When Beast galloped across the yard to greet her, his
massive head reaching almost to her waist, Julia managed to pet him without flinching. The dog licked
her hand as if he, too, wanted to part on good terms.

In the laundry room Julia bent down to retrieve
her abandoned jacket from the basket on the floor
and rolled it into a ball beneath her arm. When
she straightened and turned to leave, she gasped,
her heart racing at the shadow in the doorway;
Tony stepped forward into the light—just as he had
the night before, a lifetime ago.

Julia gave a shaky laugh and hugged her jacket
more tightly to keep from reaching for him. She
didn't think she would be able to let go. "It's kind
of spooky when you just appear like that," she said
to break the silence.

He must have known how she ached to touch
him; somehow it showed in her face or her eyes,
because Tony reached out to pull Julia into his embrace, holding her so tightly that her ear was
pressed against the beating of his heart. She held
on to him as though she were never going to leave,

clinging to him for a last time, laying unspoken claim to the feel of his muscles, to the warmth of his skin. "Julia," he whispered. She breathed it all in: the tenor of his voice, the softness of his shirt, the strength of his arms, the wonderful scent that was man and leather mixed with the great outdoors and hard work. It was a combination far headier than the scent of any expensive cologne. It was impossible that Julia could just walk away from anyone so perfect for her. She wasn't sure where she would find the courage to do it.

Tears slipped out and Julia kept her face braced against his shirt, hoping to keep the moisture in her eyes hidden until she had the unwanted emotion under control. But at the first unavoidable sniff, she felt Tony tense and he reached down to slip his fingers beneath her chin. He lifted her face to his, not allowing her to hide away the tears as she so wished. Julia was left with no way to disguise the hot tracks making their way down her cheeks.

Almost reverently, Tony caught the moisture of a single tear on the tip of his index finger, wiping away the remaining wetness that coated her cheeks. Then he leaned down and his lips followed the path the tears had forged. His kiss moved slowly, healing the sharp pain and blessing her with its soft promise. The kiss was a feather-light dusting that touched Julia's very soul before settling over her lips to drink.

And when the healing kiss finally ended and Tony drew back from her lips, Julia knew that her desire to stay had only deepened. What need did she really have in Phoenix that could outweigh the pleasure of Tony's touch, the sweetness of Tony's kiss? There could be nothing that would compare.

Julia would be content to remain cushioned forever in Tony's strong arms, pressed against a heart that pounded as rapidly as her own.

At last Tony broke the spell, letting time and harsh reality again intrude into their world. "I wish I could hold you like this all day," he said. His lips were warm against her hair as he spoke the very thoughts Julia was trying to avoid. "But I don't want to worry about you trying to get home after dark. Remember, I've seen your night landings."

A choked laugh burst out of her, pushing away the sadness of the dawning good-bye. Julia pulled back from her nest in his arms so that she could see his face; she loved the way the dimple in Tony's cheek deepened when he teased her. "I'm better when I'm not battling twenty-knot crosswinds," she said. "Besides, if it gets too late tonight to get all the way home, I suppose I could always find another big ranch to land on. I think I'm starting to like the great unknown."

The grip of Tony's hands tightened where they rested at her waist. "Another ranch, huh? Planning on making a habit of that, are you?"

"Maybe," Julia qualified, enjoying the chance to tease him in return, "but only if you'll promise to be the rancher who's waiting there to welcome me." She returned her attention to the collar of his shirt, tracing the tip of her finger lightly down across his skin to the first button. "In fact," she said, thoughtfully, "I think I like taking on reclusive ranchers with big, mean dogs. I made it past the growls and haven't been bitten once."

"Beast doesn't bite."

"I wasn't taking about Beast. I was talking about you."

"Don't be too sure about that, smartie. You have no idea how much I'd like to eat you alive."

Julia's breath caught in her throat. So much for going right home. "Surely you don't think I'm just going to leave after a line like that?"

"Well," Tony said, his smile so sexy that it should have been illegal, "I guess it's not really all that late, yet. We might have another minute or two we could spend."

He lowered his head, taking Julia's lips in a kiss that was far more than slow and seductive. It was a kiss to heat a fire that would burn all through the night, a kiss to light an ember that could never be extinguished. It was a kiss that wrapped its warmth around Julia's heart and filled her body with a deep longing, yet consoled her with promises that her every dream would somehow come true.

But for now, she knew that the kiss and the dream had come to an end and there was no way to ignore the reality any longer. The western mountains were already casting late afternoon shadows, and a career and three cats waited for her in Scottsdale.

The setting sun still radiated enough heat to soak through Julia's clothes as she automatically went through the Cessna's pre-flight check. Although she was standing in the shade of the airplane's wing, the heat seeped through the shoulders of her shirt and the legs of her jeans, reminding her that summer was well on the way. But Julia's shoulders and legs were a far cry from where she felt the heat burning the most; the sun's warmth was nothing compared to the memory of Tony's body pressed against hers.

She would probably never complain about the Arizona sun again.

As she climbed up the wing and slid into the seat, readying the airplane for take-off, Julia looked out the side window at the handsome face shaded beneath the black cowboy hat and forced herself to give him a smile instead of bursting into the tears that again threatened. Going home didn't mean she would never see him again, Julia assured herself again. Tony felt just as she did, and between them they would find a way to be together again. With just a little time, everything was going to work out.

And Julia was sure that if she repeated the words long enough, maybe her heart would begin to believe them.

There were no more tearful good-byes, no more long kisses to be shared, only a whispered promise to be safe on the flight home, and to land in Tucson if the weather changed for the worse. As the orange wind socks still showed no sign of life and only soft white clouds dotted the horizon, Julia thought that a storm was improbable, but she agreed with Tony anyway. The fact that he was worried about her was a last layer of icing on a wonderful day.

She started the engine and the propeller jumped to life, raising the noise to a level that ended all possibility of conversation. At the end of the rugged runway, Tony raised his hand and swept his dark hat off his head in a final gesture of farewell. Julia returned a brief wave before settling the headset over her ears and turning her concentration to the airplane. It was time to forget everything but flying, time to focus her attention to the first dirt strip take-off she had ever attempted.

By the time the airplane was soaring high and safe above the desert and Julia was able to look down on the ranch from her lazy circle in the air, there was no longer any sign of Tony out by the strip of runway. A mile or so away, Julia saw a long yellow school bus turn off of the highway and onto the miles of dirt road that led to the ranch.

It was only after Julia had set the airplane's heading for the route through the mountain pass and settled back for the flight that she realized she had never thought to ask Tony for his telephone number, or his address, or even which of the thousands of highway turnoffs led to his ranch.

Short of dropping out of the sky on her next visit to Buena Vista, Julia had no way of reaching him.

SEVEN

On Tuesday, Julia woke up late for work, was still exhausted, and was ready to take a whole week off. Unfortunately, she had to put in office hours all morning and rounds at the teaching hospital in the late afternoon, so even taking one more day was out of the question.

She eased her sore muscles down on one knee and put a smiley-face sticker on the blue-striped shirt of her morning's last patient. The boy rewarded her with an almost toothless grin, and Julia gave the prescription for antibiotics to his mother. She waited until the two of them had made their next appointment and had stepped outside before she walked the charts down the hall to her secretary. She was lucky enough to find Rene busy at the file cabinet with her back turned, so Julia tried to be silent as she rummaged through the piles on the desk, hoping to find a scribbled message that Tony had tried to call her. Despite the fact that Julia had left with no way of reaching him, her office number was listed in the directory, and Tony should easily be able to find it if he decided he wanted to. Julia had been hoping that he would want to.

"Are you looking for something specific I can

help you with, or did you just want to mess up my system?"

Julia jumped, immediately guilty. She had already questioned Rene twice that morning and wasn't willing to ask again. "No, not really," Julia hedged. "I was just wondering if I had any new messages."

"No new messages," Rene said slowly, studying Julia's face. Then Rene's eyes lit up with interest. "It has to be a man. That's it, isn't it? You met someone you liked at the Buena Vista clinic this weekend and now you're waiting for him to call?"

Obviously, Rene had known her far too long, and worse, she was like a bloodhound once she was on the scent. Julia scowled. "Don't be ridiculous. I'm just expecting some lab results back on Mr. Cordoba and I wanted to get them before I left for the hospital."

"You don't act like you're waiting for any lab results. You act like you're waiting for a man."

"Just forget it, Rene. It wasn't really important anyway. What I *did* want to know is if you were able to reach Frank and if you let him know I have to cancel our plans for tonight."

"Yes, and he wasn't very happy to hear it. He tried to insist on talking to you, but I told him you would be tied up for the rest of the day." Rene smirked. "I don't think he believed me." She picked up the loose stack of manila folders Julia had moved and returned the stack to the correct spot on her desk. It was obvious from Rene's attitude that she didn't really care *what* Frank believed. "I'm glad you canceled tonight," Rene continued. "Breaking it off with that pompous jerk was the best thing you ever did. What I can't understand is why you would agree to go out on even one more date with him."

"It wasn't going to be a date," Julia corrected her. "I was very clear with Frank about that point when we made these plans. But since we were both attending the same lecture it just made sense to drive into the city together."

Rene shrugged. "If you say so, Julia. Personally, I wouldn't trust Frank Leslie's motives about anything, no matter what he says. The only two things Frank really cares about are the face he kisses in the mirror every morning and whether he's going to win the election next year."

Julia laughed. Frank did spend a lot of time in front of the mirror. "I've never seen him actually kiss his reflection," she corrected.

"I'm serious, Julia. I have been telling you for ages that there are some great men out there and that you should let me set you up with someone. You could give one of my choices a try just one time—it surely can't be worse than another date with Frank. And I know some nice, available men who would love to meet you."

Julia looked at her pretty receptionist and shook her head at the suggestion. Despite Rene's attraction to big hairdos and flashy clothing, her stunningly pretty face and her voluptuous figure drew admiring male glances everywhere she went. Given any encouragement at all, men, young and old, fell at her feet. The last thing Julia needed to do was take on a string of Rene's castoffs. "If these men you know are so nice and so available, then why aren't you dating them?"

Rene set her lips in a tight line. "*My* dating is not

the point, and you know it. At least I actually date once in a while, which is more than I can say for you. Really, Julia, you can't deny it, and how will you find anyone if you never even go out? You should at least agree to meet these men." Rene turned away, but not before Julia saw her smug smile. "Then maybe you wouldn't be spending your entire morning waiting for a call from Mr. Mysterious."

Julia refused to answer. Instead, she turned and headed back into her office to finish her morning's paperwork. Rene always said what she thought and Julia had stopped arguing with her years ago. Besides, Julia *had* spent her entire morning waiting for Tony's phone call. How could she argue with the truth?

Tony still hadn't called the office by Friday evening when Julia left work for the day. Even though Julia had stopped asking days before, Rene still looked almost pitying as she gave Julia the last of the day's messages. And no wonder, Julia thought as she made her way home through the afternoon traffic snarl, she had made herself easy to pity.

It wasn't as if Tony had ever actually said at any time that he would be calling her. Julia tried to remember that and not let her disappointment ruin the memory of their day together. They had spent a wonderful time, a night and a day Julia swore she would continue to treasure, no matter the eventual outcome of her relationship with Tony. It was just that she had gone too far in her imagination, painting herself a lovely picture of phone calls and meetings and stolen moments spent in his arms; a picture that obviously in no way reflected the truth. She had flown her airplane blithely out of Tony's ranch and Tony's life, believing they might have a future together, but once gone, Julia knew she was as unmissed as she had been uninvited.

The Friday evening rush hour crawled forward like a ponderous beast, a mechanical nightmare of blaring car horns, blinking brake lights, and angry gestures. The weather was turning hotter with the dawning of summer, and the air in the city was thick with a clogging haze of floating dust and exhaust fumes. Julia nudged her car another inch forward through the traffic jam, and dreamed of being somewhere far away from the mindless fury of the other drivers, far from the constant stress of the bumper-to-bumper traffic. She needed to be someplace calm and serene, a place she could hear the wind blow through the desert. She wanted to be where the trees reached to the dome of clear sky and hawks circled high above it all, their calls echoing in the vast emptiness. She wanted to be in a place where she could see for miles, and not have another house or car or human being to block her view. She wanted a place like Tony's ranch.

There it was again, just as it had been all week. Eventually, every damned thing Julia did reminded her of Tony.

When Julia finally made it safely into her driveway and unlocked the door to her small apartment, the flashing light on her message machine made her heart speed up with the dying hope that perhaps Tony had called at last. But even that tiny hope died when Rene's voice came across the tape, calling with a reminder that she would be by on Sunday afternoon to ride with Julia to the press conference. Julia didn't really want to go, but it would be a big media event with Hands Across the Border as the focus. With any luck, the reporters who attended would be interested enough to do a story on the clinic itself, and free publicity was too good a thing to turn down.

The telephone rang a second time as Julia was carrying in her groceries from the car. She caught it on the third ring, just before it flipped to the answering machine.

"Hello? Wait! Damn." Juggling the bags in her arms, Julia dropped the telephone on the floor. The tangled wire coiled around her foot like a snake determined to hold on. Dragging the receiver behind her, Julia hobbled the last few steps to the dining room table to set down her groceries before they fell, too. She had to slip off her high heel to get the phone unwound from her foot.

With Julia's luck, the person had probably hung up by now.

"Hello?"

"Julia?"

There was no mistaking that gorgeous deep voice. Julia forgot all about the groceries. "Tony, I am so glad you called."

"Hi, honey. It's good to hear your voice. I tried to reach you at your office, but the secretary said you had already left for home. Where did you find that girl anyway? Scotland Yard? I practically had to fax her my birth certificate to get your home telephone number, and it took me a good thirty minutes to talk her into giving it to me. "

That was so like Rene that Julia smiled. "Rene's been trying to claw the details about meeting you out of me all week and I wouldn't tell her much of anything. Getting to actually talk to you probably made her whole day."

Tony's laugh was so sexy that even over the phone it gave Julia the shivers. "Well I'm glad she's enjoying it," Tony said, " 'cause anything that much trouble should be fun for one of us." He was silent for a long minute, then added, "I sure have missed you this week, Julia."

"Then why did you wait five days to call?" Julia bit her lip. The words had escaped before she could stop them. She had practiced what she would say to him at least a hundred times, and always the words had been cool and aloof, not heated and accusing—not proving that she had been counting each long day as it passed without his phone call.

But Tony's voice remained warm and familiar. "I'm sorry, honey. I haven't had much of a chance to call you sooner. My son's horse, Kareem, came down with colic Monday evening, and it's been pretty crazy around the ranch since then. Every time I made it inside the house to telephone, I'd get the message that your office was already closed for the day. Besides, it was probably too late at night to bother you anyway."

The hurt and tension she had carried inside all week lifted from her shoulders. Here was a reason Julia could understand; when your life was already busy, a problem like a sick horse could become all-consuming. "You wouldn't have bothered me," she assured him. "No matter how late it was. How is Kareem now?"

"Oh, the horse is going to be fine. By Wednesday

afternoon, he was out of the woods and my son was able to take over his care, but by then, it seemed like I'd never catch up with the three days of chores we'd had to put off."

"And after you wasted all day Monday, too," Julia said.

Tony was quick to contradict her. "Monday definitely wasn't wasted. In fact, it was the best day I have spent all year," he said. "I really mean that, Julia. I had a great time being with you."

"Me, too. I had a great time with you, too. I didn't realize until I was in the air that I had no way of reaching you, not even a telephone number."

"I know, although that didn't occur to me until late Tuesday night. And it's been driving me crazy that I couldn't call you, couldn't talk to you. Yesterday, I almost gave up getting hold of you in person. I was seriously thinking of asking your answering service if I could see you this weekend."

He wanted to see her this weekend! Julia leaped out of her chair. But jumping in the air was a bad idea while wearing only one high heel, and she landed off-balance. Julia tumbled back into the chair at her desk and the chair rolled away with her in it, gliding to the limit of the phone cord before Julia grabbed the edge of the desk to stop. Then she remembered the fund-raiser and all of her elation drained away. She pulled herself back next to the desk and rested her head in her hand. "Oh, Tony, I can't fly down this weekend, as much as I would like to. I have a dinner I have to attend on Sunday—well, a press conference really. I don't even want to go, but it's been in the works a long time and there's no way I can get out of it." Julia stopped. She was rambling again; even she could hear it.

"Julia?"

"Yes?"

"I understand."

But she didn't believe him. "I'd honestly rather be spending the weekend with you, there at your ranch," she said. "I already know that the dinner isn't going to be any fun, but I have to be there."

"Actually, Julia, I wasn't going to ask you to fly down here anyway. I'm going to be driving my daughter up to the mall at Casa Grande tomorrow and I was hoping that you wouldn't mind spending part of your day there with the two of us. I'll tell you up front, though, that Angela's prom is coming up and she needs to shop for a dress. And she's not all that keen on having my help picking it out, not that I really blame her. To tell you the truth, I'm fairly awful at that sort of thing and she knows it. I figured that if you were along to throw in your opinion, maybe she'd be willing to listen to it."

Julia laughed at Tony's candid admission. He was clearly very good at handling his teenage daughter. "I would love to go shopping with the two of you tomorrow," she said. "And I think that it's very sweet of you to drive Angela all the way to Casa Grande just for a shopping trip. Angela is one lucky girl to have a parent like you."

"Angela is one picky girl," Tony corrected. "She's already dragged me to all the women's clothing stores around this area. What she would really like is for me to chauffeur her all the way to Rodeo Drive for the weekend, but I told her that the trip to the outlet mall is as far as I am willing to go."

"I'm sure we'll be able to find something she likes at the mall. I know I could."

"And if you are going to be there, then I'm sure to find something I like, too."

The words Julia had been craving. "Pretty words," she said lightly.

"No, honey, I'm just being honest." Tony waited a heartbeat, as if he could feel her smile through the telephone wire. "I guess we'll be seeing you tomorrow morning in Casa Grande then," he said. "Angela and I will get an early start, and we'll meet you at ten o'clock in front of that big clothing store on the west end."

"I'll be waiting for you."

"Sounds good, honey. Then I'll see you tomorrow."

"Bye, Tony," Julia whispered. She could hardly wait and she knew she wouldn't be able to sleep. This would be their first real date.

Saturday morning, the traffic on the highway leaving Phoenix was light and Julia was able to reach the outlet mall in record time. Since she had left the house early to begin with, she had plenty of time to brush her hair for the thousandth time and chastise herself for her newfound vanity.

Even worse, she had spent hours that morning agonizing over what to wear when she met Tony and his daughter. Normally, Julia could be completely dressed, out the door, and to the office within thirty minutes of waking up, but today she had already tried on at least twelve different outfits before she finally settled on the dark blue skirt with the butterfly belt and the matching white T-shirt with its low scalloped neck. She told herself that the indecision was understandable; the only time Tony had seen her, she'd been wearing jeans and a ragged sweater for two whole days, and was mostly wet or covered with hay the entire time she was there. This time, Julia was determined to at least look better.

At ten minutes past the appointed hour, the enormous parking lot at the outlet mall was filling up fast, but there was still no sign of Tony's blue truck in the crowd of cars turning off of the highway. Julia walked once more along the sidewalk in front of the Liz Claiborne store and wondered how long she should wait. With a three-hour drive to make, there was no telling what delays Tony and his daughter might have run into; their car could have even broken down, or they might have had a flat tire. Ten more minutes—then she'd buy a soda and settle in comfortably. Julia was willing to wait all day if it meant a chance to be with Tony for a few hours.

"Julia!"

Shading her eyes with her hand, Julia turned toward the morning sun, her gaze searching the turn-off from the highway. Her hand fell to her side and the welcoming smile on her lips turned to a low whistle when a white Jaguar pulled up at her side and the tinted window slid all the way down.

"I was expecting the pickup truck," she said. "This is quite an upgrade." That was an enormous understatement. As ignorant as she was about expensive automobiles, Julia still knew this one was a classic.

Tony's eyes were hidden behind dark Ray Ban sunglasses, but it was the same sexy smile. He leaned back against the leather seat so that Julia could see across to the passenger side. "Julia this is my troublesome daughter, Angela—the one who insisted that we weren't bringing the truck today. Angela, this is Dr. Julia Huerta, the lady I was telling you about."

"It's nice to meet you, Dr. Huerta."

"Please, call me Julia. It's nice to meet you, too, Angela." Tony's daughter looked younger than sixteen, despite her obvious attempts to look exactly the opposite. Her skin was naturally pale beneath her dark hair, and the slashes of color that passed for blush were garish on her young face. Still, her smile was sweet and Julia could hear the nervousness behind the shy words she offered. Julia was nervous, too. Maybe Angela hadn't really wanted her to come along. Maybe she didn't want to share her father with a stranger.

"I can't wait to go shopping," Julia said, pushing aside any uneasiness. "I've been looking forward to it all night. Why don't you park the car and let's get started."

Tony's glance at his daughter lasted a full second. His fingers tapped the dashboard. He cleared his throat. "Well," he said, "I think I'll just let Angela out here and you two can get started shopping while I take care of a few things I need to do. I'll catch up with you girls in the store a little later."

With a nod, Angela opened the car's passenger door and climbed out. She shrugged her way up to the sidewalk, with her wide bell-bottoms nearly covering her tall platform shoes. When Tony pulled the Jaguar away to park, Angela looked so uncomfortable and so abandoned, Julia's heart went out to her.

"Let's go on inside the store and have a look around. There's no sense waiting around for your dad. Men aren't any help with this kind of thing anyway."

"Yeah," Angela said, with an appraising glance at the parking lot. "We should go in. I don't think Dad will be coming inside anytime soon."

In fact, Angela was right. Tony didn't show up while they were inside that first store at all, and he didn't come into the second one, either. By the time Julia and Angela left the third clothing store, it had been well over two hours since Tony had said good-bye and driven off in his white Jaguar, its opaque windows tightly closed. It wasn't until Julia and Angela had already walked through more than half of the long mall and had stopped for a bite to eat that they saw Tony coming out of the men's room. He was carrying a newspaper, and he was nearly hidden behind it as he walked. If it weren't for Angela, Julia wouldn't have even see him.

"Hi, Dad."

The newspaper dropped no more than an inch. His sunglasses gleamed at them. "Hi, Angela. Hi, Julia. How is the shopping going?"

How is the shopping going? Maybe he should have joined them as he'd promised; then Tony would have known for himself. Surely, Julia thought, no one could be that dense. She wanted to hit him over the head with something very heavy, but unfortunately, all she had was her purse—and there were no bricks inside. "The shopping is going fine. Just fine." No thanks to him. Julia's words were clipped with anger. She waited for Tony to offer them an apology.

"Good, I'm glad." Tony flashed them that gorgeous smile. "Then how about if I meet you at three o'clock back on the sidewalk where we started? That gives you three more hours, which should be more than enough time, don't you think?" And that was it, end of conversation. He simply said, "See you there," and walked away, newspaper held high, and never even looked Julia in the eye.

Anger and hurt warred within her, and Julia blinked back the stupid tears that threatened. Tony had explained to her last night that she would be shopping with Angela. Julia had just assumed that he would be with them—that Tony wanted to spend time with her. She had obviously been mistaken.

A small, light hand came to rest on Julia's shoulder, a child offering comfort for the parent's bad behavior. "We don't have to shop for the dress anymore today," Angela told her gently. "Not if you don't want to. I can wait until another day."

Julia turned around to face the teenager and felt some of her stiff anger drain away. Angela's dark eyes were solemn beneath her blue eye shadow and heavy mascara, and worry for Julia etched an unnatural line in her young forehead. Something was definitely wrong with the father, but the daughter was very sweet and considerate—and in need of a little guidance, which Julia could provide. She took a deep, cleansing breath, pushing away the anger. "There's no way I'm leaving here yet," Julia said. She covered Angela's hand with her own and gave it a gentle squeeze. "Somewhere in this mall is a perfect prom dress made just for you. And I'm not leaving here until we find it."

Angela's relief was obvious. She was probably starved for attention, and no wonder. The least Julia could do was give the girl this one special day.

"Forget the lunch," Julia said, studying the menus that lined the walls of the cafeteria. "Let's go straight to the ice cream."

She and Angela had plenty in common, and they didn't need Tony to have fun. They would have a great time all on their own.

"You really blew it today, Dad."

Tony glanced at his daughter. She was leaning back against the Jaguar's leather seat, pale arms folded dramatically across her chest. One look at her expression and Tony felt more like an erring child than the parent, which was, no doubt, what Angela had intended. "I don't know what I could have done differently back there, Angela. Every damned time I tried to get out of the car it was crazy. You know how it gets some days. I was lucky to make it inside to use the bathroom. The next time you want to go shopping we take the damned truck. At least it doesn't draw so much attention."

But Angela wasn't about to be sidetracked. "You could have told her the truth. You *should* have told her the truth. I almost told her myself." Angela sighed and shifted in the seat so that she was facing him, and her voice turned pleading. "Julia is awfully nice, Dad, and I think she would understand if you would just trust her. She's not like the other women you've dated; she even talked to me like a grown-up. Then, we found the greatest formal in the last store and she even helped me pick out some new makeup."

Tony smiled to himself. He had noticed his daughter's trademark blue eye shadow was missing, but hadn't wanted to mention it. "You look real pretty with the new makeup, honey. You and Julia did a good job."

"And Julia helped me pick out the perfect name for my horse, too. I've decided I'm going to call him Maximillian. Julia said it has to be a strong name to go with his ancestors and that I should choose a name with a lot of history behind it. She said that when I take Maximillian into the competition ring, the judges will read his name out over the loudspeaker and all the people in the stands will turn to see him."

The competition ring. His daughter was interested in riding in the competition ring. Tony felt like he'd been offered a miracle. "The name is wonderful," Tony said.

"*Julia* is wonderful," Angela prompted.

"I completely agree with you."

"Then what are you going to do about it? You have to do *something* after today."

The crossed arms returned, as his daughter demanded an answer. But what to do about it was the one question Tony didn't have an answer for. Angela was right; he had blown it.

When Tony had returned to pick up Angela in the parking lot of the shopping center, and had seen Julia again, she had looked angry, bewildered and hurt. All Tony had wanted to do was sweep her into his arms and carry her away until he could make her smile again. But there had been no time to do anything besides thank her for helping Angela and say a very quick good-bye. Julia had never noticed the growing crowd on the sidewalk, but Angela and Tony had.

"You're right, I should have told her. I'll call her tonight and explain."

"You'd better start thinking up an awfully good explanation. I think you're going to need one."

"I'll just tell her the truth," Tony said. "And I'll send her some flowers."

Angela was watching him. She'd had the same look that morning—when she'd talked him into driving the Jaguar. It was a look that generally meant trouble; Tony knew that from experience.

"What?"

"I think you should do something a lot bigger than just sending Julia some flowers. Anyone can send flowers. But you need to do something special, something that will be sure to really impress her."

Tony almost hated to ask. "Exactly what *something* did you have in mind?"

Angela nonchalantly brushed her dark bangs from her eyes and twisted the silver rings on her fingers before continuing. "Julia said that she has an important dinner to go to tomorrow night. That's why she can't come with us to the ranch for a visit."

"I know."

"The dinner is to plan the fund-raiser for the clinic she works at. And for them to decide on who will be the entertainment."

"No." Tony's fingers tightened around the leather steering wheel.

"Don't say 'no.' It's just a little concert. It would be fun."

"No."

"But, Dad! Just think how grateful Julia would be if you agreed. If you told her you would do it, she'd forgive you for sure—for everything!"

"I haven't *done* anything." Tony willed himself to keep his voice calm. "Forget it, Angela. There's no way I'm opening myself, and all of us, up for that kind of crap again. Things are just starting to settle down in our lives. There's absolutely no way I'm going to go through it again."

Angela was so mad that she turned forward and remained silent, but Tony didn't think that would last. Angela wasn't one to keep her temper to herself, and she still had three whole hours to nag at him. It was going to be a long drive home.

EIGHT

She had been a fool to expect so much; she'd set herself up for the disappointment and there was no one else to blame.

Knowing it didn't make Julia feel any better.

After all the hours she had spent planning for Saturday, and picking out what to wear, and driving down to Casa Grande to meet him, Tony hadn't bothered to spend even a single minute in her company while she was there. In fact, when Julia finally did see Tony again that afternoon in the mall's parking lot, he'd hurriedly grabbed his daughter and driven away without even looking back. He had barely a word to spare for Julia. It could not have been any clearer how he felt.

When her front doorbell rang on Sunday afternoon, Julia was in the shower, trying to get herself ready in time for the promotional dinner. Turning off the shower, Julia dripped her way across the bathroom, yanked open the door and hollered, "Just a minute," before running across the hall to her bedroom for her robe. "This had better be awfully important," Julia muttered as she pulled the robe closed and stalked her way to the front door. If it was Frank out there, he was thirty minutes early and Julia was darned well going to tell him to wait outside. She hadn't wanted to drive to the dinner with him in the first place, but Frank had talked her into it, saying she owed him for backing out on the lecture the other night. Julia had finally stopped arguing and agreed to drive there in his car. Then she had promptly invited Rene to join them.

Julia was prepared to face Frank, prepared to give him a piece of her mind, but when she answered the door it was something much worse than Frank that greeted her: It was a dozen long-stemmed roses.

Frank obviously hadn't understood the part about the night not being a date.

Julia signed for the flowers and carried them inside, where she had to shove two of her cats off of the dining room table to make room for the tall, cut-crystal vase. It was evident that no expense had been spared in ordering the elaborate arrangement, and *that* was so unlike Frank that it actually made her nervous. Although they were beautiful, Julia was already dreading the fact that she would have to thank Frank for them later.

Julia found the small square envelope with the florist's logo tucked deep inside the dark green leaves. Pulling out the plastic spike that held it in place, she took out the card and her gaze skimmed to the bottom.

Love, Tony.

The flowers were from Tony.

Suddenly the delivery held a whole other meaning. A dozen long-stemmed red roses in a crystal vase was a wonderful gift. Maybe it meant that Tony was sorry, or maybe he'd been ill, or maybe he had discovered that he simply couldn't live without her and was begging her to see him again. The envelope and card slipped from Julia's fingers and floated down to the carpet and she plopped down in a seat beside them. Pushing back her still-dripping hair so that she wouldn't get the precious card wet, Julia picked up the envelope and pulled out the note. Something inside her still hoped. . . .

"Thank you for taking Angela shopping. It was great to see you again. I'll call you later. Tony."

And that was it. There were no declarations of undying love, no apologies for the day they hadn't spent together, and certainly no request that they try meeting again on another day. Julia was old enough to recognize a good-bye when she saw one. It was past time to stop kidding herself.

The grandfather clock at the end of the hall sounded four dour tones and Julia's heart echoed the sound. Getting to her feet, she tucked the card inside the pocket of her robe and headed back for the bathroom to finish dressing. She only had thirty minutes left to get ready for the dinner. There was no more time to spend dreaming about a gorgeous man she would probably never see again.

She barely heard the sound of the doorbell over the blow dryer's roar.

Still not ready, Julia tied the bathrobe tighter around her waist and ran to the door again. This time when she looked through the peephole, it was indeed Frank who was waiting outside. He was dressed, as always, in a conservative blue suit with wide lapels, a dark blue-and-black-striped tie and a white shirt with monogrammed cuffs. On his feet, Frank sported his trademark wingtip shoes—they'd gained him a lot of attention with the press—and in Frank's hand was a single red rose wrapped in florist tissue.

Julia silently turned the lock on the front door and ran back to the bathroom before calling for him to come in. When she heard the door close again, Julia locked the bathroom door and reached for the black dress she planned to wear. She didn't want to spend any more time alone with Frank than she had to, and she prayed Rene would show up soon.

But when Julia had dawdled as long as possible getting ready and finally walked out of the bathroom, Rene still hadn't arrived. Frank was standing beside the dining room table, his single drooping rose lying abandoned beside the dozen glorious blooms in the vase, and in his hand he held the empty green envelope from the florist shop. Julia was suddenly very glad that she had tucked Tony's card safely away.

"Who sent you the roses?" Frank's usually smooth voice was angry and possessive—which he certainly had no right to be. Frank had no claim on her beyond friendship and he damned well knew it. Julia had been more than clear on that point.

"The flowers are from a friend of mine. No one you know," Julia said shortly, turning away. It was all the explanation she planned to give him, and already more than she had intended to say. "It's time to leave and I'm almost ready. We just need to wait for Rene to get here." Julia picked up her small black purse from the couch.

Frank crushed the green envelope in his fist

and the collapse of the stiff paper crackled through the small room. "Julia, are you seeing someone besides me?"

Julia threw up her hands and turned around to face him. "Frank, for the last time, I'm not *seeing* you. We tried it, it didn't work out, and now it's over. You said you wanted to attend this dinner together, that it would be good for your publicity. Fine—feel free to get your picture in the paper. But who sends me roses is really none of your business."

Frank took a conciliatory step toward her, his face softening into a contrite mask, his tone turning wheedling. "I want very much to make it my business, Julia. I thought I had made that fact clear to you. I know I made some mistakes with you before, but I want you to give me another chance. If we could just try again, you and I could be a perfect team. You could be the woman at my side when I win the campaign."

"Forget it." Julia had heard more than enough. She wasn't interested in politics and she certainly wasn't interested in being the woman at Frank's side. Turning away from him, Julia stepped into her black high heels. "You'll have to win that campaign alone, Frank. The *us* thing isn't going to happen."

This time, when the doorbell chimed, Julia welcomed the interruption. Frank reached the door first and jerked it open with a force that surely strained the hinges. From outside on the step, Rene beamed in at them, a ridiculous pink bow hanging askew from her hair. She wore a blue pants suit with wide lapels that looked suspiciously like Frank's own and black-and-white wingtips that were exactly like Frank's.

"I hope I'm not too late," Rene said. "I had a heck of a time finding the right shoes."

Rene looked from Frank's stony expression to Julia's angry one, and her eyes darkened with interest. Frank didn't stop to say another word to either of them. Leaving the house, he almost knocked Rene out of her wingtips as he pushed past her, and once inside his car, he slammed the door closed. The chrome wheel rims on Frank's sports car spun wildly as he put the car in reverse, hit the accelerator, and squealed out of the driveway.

"Well, that takes care of one problem." With an airy wave to the disappearing car, Rene stepped inside Julia's apartment and pushed the door closed behind her. Her gaze went immediately to the roses sitting on the table and the crumpled envelope lying abandoned on the floor. Reaching down, Rene picked up the envelope and smoothed it out in her hands. She managed to keep her expression completely serious as she looked up at Julia. "I gather the roses aren't from Frank," she said.

It was too much for Julia. Her sense of humor erupted. The tension from Tony's note coupled with Frank's demanding reaction had left her nerves tightly strung, but with Rene, that tension escaped into giggles. Rene grinned, and in a minute she was laughing, too. The two of them leaned against the wall, unable even to hold each other up as their laughter bubbled out until tears filled their eyes. "Well," Julia finally managed to say, "Frank did bring the one rose on the table."

Rene looked at the single, drooping rose resting next to the gorgeous dozen in the elegant vase and it sent her off again into fresh laughter. Julia and

Rene were both still giggling as they opened the front door to leave. "I guess we won't get to take a ride in Frank's fancy sports car after all," Julia said. "And here I thought we'd make a grand entrance."

"Guess not. Sorry about that," Rene said, but she didn't sound like she was really sorry at all. "Do you want to drive to the dinner or shall I?"

"You drive. You're dressed just like Frank anyway. I'll just pretend I'm in a sports car."

Rene looked down proudly at her blue suit and wingtips. "Do you think he noticed?"

Julia figured they were lucky to get out of the house in time to be only a little bit late.

"So?"

Julia glanced over. "So, what?" She'd wondered how long it would take Rene to start with the questions. Actually, she had lasted longer than Julia would have given her credit for.

"Give it up, Julia. I want all the details, so spill."

"Watch the road." They weren't in any real danger. Julia knew very well that Rene was capable of doing a thousand things at once—that was what made her such a great secretary and why Julia didn't have to hire anyone else. Rene was a whole staff in one tiny dynamo.

Julia's "staff" tapped her red-lacquered nails impatiently against the steering wheel of her Sunbird as she waited for the light to change. "All right. I suppose the name of the person who sent you the beautiful roses is really none of my business, and that you don't have to tell me a thing about the mystery man you've been pining over all this week.

But I'm not going to let that worry me. There's always next week to get you to talk. Let's see . . . we'll be in the office all day together on Monday, and Tuesday, and we're working late on Wednesday. . . ."

"That's blackmail."

"That's right," Rene said smugly.

"And I haven't been pining over him."

Rene pounced. "I knew it! It's the man who called the office on Friday, isn't it? What a great voice he has; just talking to him gave me the shivers. Where did you meet him? At the clinic last weekend? Is he as sexy as he sounds?"

"I should take out an ad in the newspaper," Julia grumbled. "It's really not a big deal, Rene. Can't you just leave it alone?"

"No, I cannot just leave it alone," Rene answered matter-of-factly. "Someone needs to be concerned about your love life, as Lord knows you certainly don't seem to be. At least you didn't seem to be up until last week," she qualified, casting Julia an appraising glance.

"No one needs to worry about my love life, and it's really no more your business than it was Frank's."

"Oh, please, spare me. But I'm just going to ignore the fact that you just compared me to Frank. Anyway, I know you; you're just trying to start an argument and change the subject, but I'm not going to let you. Now stop your stalling and tell me everything about last weekend and this man you met in Buena Vista. Don't leave anything out."

There were too darned many stoplights in downtown Phoenix. Rene could make the inquisition last forever. Julia tried one more tactic, although she already knew that she was doomed. "I don't know all that much about him. You talked to him. You probably already know more than I do," she said.

Rene groaned. "Don't be so evasive. Start with the simple stuff, like what is his name? Where did you meet him? Heavens, the man is as secretive as you are. I couldn't get him to tell me anything over the phone."

"And I'll bet you tried," Julia said. Then she gave in to the inevitable. She would tell Rene at least part of the truth about the weekend, but there were some moments Julia was definitely going to leave out; Rene didn't need to know *everything*. "His name is Tony, and I didn't meet him in Buena Vista. I met him at his ranch on the way home from the clinic last weekend." That was obviously not what Rene had expected. She stared so long she had to slam on the brakes at the next stoplight.

"Would you please watch the road?" Julia complained. "You're going to kill us."

"What were you doing at his ranch?"

"There was a bad storm Sunday evening when I was flying home, so I saw his runway and landed. That's all there is to it."

"That's all there is to it?" Rene repeated. Julia was beginning to be thankful for the stoplights; maybe having Rene drive to the dinner wasn't such a great idea after all. "When you called me Sunday evening," Rene said, "I thought you were stuck in some small-town airport overnight, probably forced to sleep on some ratty old couch. Instead, you tell me that you dropped out of the sky and landed in some gorgeous rancher's arms where you spent a long enchanted weekend, and you say, 'That's all there is to it'?"

"I never said he was gorgeous."

Rene laughed so hard she snorted. "You didn't have to say anything, Julia," she managed to choke out. "I was the one who had to listen to you sigh around the office all week, remember?"

"I did *not* sigh around the office all week."

"And he's a rancher? Does that mean he grows cows?"

"Yes. He raises cattle."

"Cattle? La-di-da, how rich. Miss Julia has found herself a cattle baron. So, why did the baron wait all the way until Friday night to finally call you?"

When Julia didn't answer the question right away, Rene turned her attention from the road once again. "He did call you on Friday, didn't he? He certainly talked me out of your home number smoothly enough."

Julia nodded reluctantly. "He called me on Friday. Yesterday I drove down and met him in Casa Grande. He asked me to help his daughter pick out a prom dress at the mall."

"And you didn't even tell me about this?"

"Give me a break, Rene. This is the first time I've see you since then."

"You could have used the telephone." Rene returned her attention to the road, but the pout didn't leave her lower lip. "And today he sent you a dozen roses?"

"Yes, but it's not what you think. He sent the flowers simply to thank me for going shopping with his daughter. It sure as heck wasn't because he enjoyed being with us. In Casa Grande, Tony didn't even bother to spend any time in the stores; it was just his daughter and me all day. I guess he must have thought better about the whole date thing, decided it was a mistake. I doubt I'll ever be seeing him again."

"Julia, you were at a mall," Rene said, as though that explained everything. *"No* man likes to shop."

"It was more than just not liking to shop. It was almost like Tony was avoiding me the entire day, or like he was hiding from someone else that was there." Julia fumbled for the right words. "I don't know how to describe it, Rene. It was just plain weird. But I'm not going to worry about it anymore. It's over."

"Hmmph." Rene turned her attention back to the road. She was silent so long that Julia thought maybe she would drop the subject.

No such luck.

"Well, now I'm certainly sorry I let him get your phone number out of me," Rene complained. "How dare he have you drive all the way to Casa Grande and then not spend any time with you while you were there? The least the man could have done was to have taken you out to dinner afterward."

Julia reached across the seat and squeezed Rene's arm, grateful for her friend's support. It was nice to know that Rene was there, that there was always someone on her side. "It's not important. Don't get so angry about it that you run us off the road," she said lightly.

"This isn't funny, Julia, and it *is* important. That man is perfect for you."

"That's absurd. Besides, how would you know? You've never even met him."

"It doesn't matter whether I've met him or not. I've known you almost five years now, and I've never seen you as happy as you were on Tuesday. You were positively glowing at the office. Now, I want you to start at the beginning and tell me about every single minute you spent with this mystery man. Maybe I can figure out what went wrong."

By the time they pulled into the community center where the dinner was being held and Rene eased her car into a parking place, Julia had repeated the story of her weekend at the ranch and Tony's strange behavior in the outlet mall twice. She could almost see Rene's mind racing with plans to find out more.

"Maybe he's really a fugitive from the law and didn't want to take a chance on being recognized. Of course, anyone that owns that much land has to be known in the area, so I'm sure we can find out something about him. Tomorrow morning, we can call the Wilcox Chamber of Commerce and ask."

"Rene, don't you think you're getting a little carried away?"

"Not at all. We have to find out who he is before you see him again. What if there really is something dangerous in this guy's past? He could be a serial killer, or a bank robber. He could have been released from prison just last month for all you know."

"Don't be ridiculous. He has two kids, and it was obvious that they've all been living on the ranch for years." Not to mention that Tony was one of the gentlest men Julia had ever met. Serial killer was definitely out of the question. "And, anyway, I won't be seeing him again, so it doesn't matter."

Rene looked dubious as they pushed through

the double doors that led to the ballroom. "There has to be a way to find out more about him somehow. You certainly can't go and marry a man with a questionable past."

"Marry . . . ? Rene, are you out of your mind? I have no intention of marrying anyone." Julia's words turned to a whisper as they pushed through the double doors and were swept into the crush of people crowded inside the Community Center Ballroom.

Rene squeezed her arm once before disappearing into the crowd. "Trust me," she whispered. "I'll find out something." Then she was gone before Julia could argue.

The publicity galas were the reason the clinic stayed in business, and once inside the ballroom, Julia was immediately pulled into the introductions that she endured twice a year to help raise contributions. Julia considered the dinners embarrassing necessities, and she always attended and always wished she could somehow avoid it. The dinners were a chance to show off the good deeds of those who contributed their time and to publicly laud the philanthropists who gave the money to keep the clinic in business. There would be prepared press releases from the Hands Across the Border governing committee, and a dozen or more journalists were already circling the room, asking questions and trying to get interviews. The news people always wanted more, always wanted to find that special angle for their story, and Julia and the five other doctors who volunteered their time would be front and center.

Finally Julia was able to work her way through the crowd to the round VIP table in front. To her surprise and disgust, she'd been given the seat right next to Frank's, and by the way he was smiling, she knew exactly who had planned it.

"I'm glad you were able to make it, darling," Frank said, standing to pull out her chair. He laid a heavy, possessive hand on her shoulder as he seated her and took the opportunity to run his fingers once through her hair in a soft caress before moving away.

Julia smiled tightly as she took her seat and managed to not jerk away from his touch. But when Frank sat down beside her at the table, she hit his knee beneath the long cloth and leaned close to his ear so that he couldn't miss her words. "Don't you ever do that to me again, Frank Leslie," she hissed. "I am *not* your darling and you can keep your hands off."

Frank's smile thinned to an angry line, but his public image was all-important to him and flashbulbs were popping, so Julia doubted he would argue. When she moved her chair a few inches away from his so that not even their knees would be in contact, Frank kept his distance.

The group was called to order as Victoria Chavez, the head of the clinic's governing committee, stepped up behind the podium and tapped twice on the microphone. The cacophony of voices grew quieter, but the movement increased as heads turned her way and the guests rearranged their seats to get a better view. Victoria waited imperiously until all chairs stopped moving and all the talking stopped; only then did she smile in acknowledgment of their attention. Julia and the other members of Hands Across the Border waited indulgently. Victoria was terribly shallow in some respects, but she worked hard for the clinic and was a natural at dealing with the press, something few of the others had the time or patience to do. If, in return, Victoria wanted to be reigning queen at the yearly conference, it was a small price to pay.

"Good evening, honored guests and members of the press." Victoria was onstage and it was obvious that she loved it; each wave of her hands was a calculated gesture to draw attention. "First, I would like to thank all of you for joining us this evening as we review another rewarding year spent working for the Hands Across the Border clinic. And, even more importantly, to finalize the plans for our upcoming fund-raiser."

She made the announcement with such enthusiasm, that there was a scattering of light applause when she finished. Victoria nodded, accepting the applause as her due, and waiting until it stopped and the room was again quiet before continuing.

"Before we get started with the real business," Virginia said, "we want to provide our guests with a brief background on the clinic's founding and subsequent success. And, tonight, it is my great pleasure to welcome our guest speaker here to do just that. He is a person I'm certain most of you already know, and I'm sure you'll all agree how very lucky we are to have someone of this man's prestige to help in our cause." She let the sentence hang with importance. "Let me introduce a man with a proven personal interest in the issues of both border health care and the indigent worker population, a man who has worked tirelessly in the clinic's interest, and a man whose deeds put him among the clinic's most dedicated benefactors." Victoria beamed at the audience before giving away the secret. "Everyone, please help me to welcome this evening's special guest speaker, Senatorial candidate Frank Leslie."

Frank stood and smiled and Julia wondered briefly how he had managed to pull it off, but she wasn't really surprised. You could always trust Frank to find the maximum camera exposure. He'd probably written Victoria's glowing introduction himself.

With the grace and the winning smile that had made him his hopeful party's candidate, Frank assumed his place behind the podium and thanked Victoria for the warm welcome. Unfolding his notes, Frank kept his attention focused on the reporters seated at the back of the room and his voice swelled with importance as he read the introductions of the clinic staff. Surely the Nobel Peace Prize was awarded with no less seriousness. The tones that had helped Frank make the jump from practicing lawyer to well-known politician held the small audience in thrall, and Frank used it to his advantage, moving his gaze from table to table, drawing everyone in. Frank spoke of the clinic's benevolent mission as though he himself had recognized the need for the organization and had worked tirelessly to bring it about—although to Julia's knowledge, he had not contributed an hour of time before that day. But despite his pompous attitude and her own personal anger at the man, Julia had to admit that Frank did make a surprisingly good choice as speaker. Besides his practiced appeal to the audience, he had obviously done his homework on the clinic's financial history, and his dynamic way of speaking had the reporters scribbling down every word.

And anything that worked for publicity worked for the clinic.

Then there was a flurry of movement behind the stage and Frank was interrupted in mid-sentence as Victoria rushed back onto the stage. The candidate's rehearsed smile quickly replaced his obvious confusion as Victoria stepped in front of him and dramatically took the microphone.

"Ladies and gentlemen, please excuse the interruption."

Left with no choice, Frank moved aside and Victoria assumed his place behind the podium. Her dramatic entrance had certainly gained everyone's attention.

"I have a very exciting and unexpected announcement to make," she said mysteriously. "Some news has just come to me that I simply must share with all of you right away. I know you're going to be as thrilled as I am." Victoria placed a chubby, beringed hand on either side of the wooden podium, and the grip of her long fingernails emphasized her excitement.

"As most of you know, the managing committee for Hands Across the Border has, for some time, been seeking to settle the question of who will be this year's entertainment for our clinic's annual fund-raiser, the Summer Night program. Unfortunately, as donations haven't been all that we had hoped, and due to some financial constraints we have been unable to resolve, the board had decided that we would need to settle for a smaller name as our main draw. In fact, tentative suggestions of local groups were already being discussed. But thanks to a phone call I received only a few moments ago, that is no longer the case. Hands Across the Border has secured a major star for the performance. I know you will all agree that our Summer Night fund-raiser is a guaranteed success." Victoria paused long enough for all eyes to look her way and the soft clicking of the cameras to begin.

"Ladies and gentlemen, Arizona's own world-renowned son, Antonio Carrera, has agreed to come out of retirement for one show and one show only. The Hands Across the Border Summer Night fund-raiser."

The effect of her announcement on the gathering was electric. Cheers and applause drowned out the rest of Victoria's words as the audience rose to its feet in excitement. Reporters shouted questions above the melee, flashbulbs pulsed as one continuous strobe, backs were slapped and general elation reigned among all those who had devoted so much to the success of the clinic. Of the entire crowd, only Julia stayed seated. Only Julia remained frozen into place.

How could she not have known?

Antonio. Antonio Carrera. The renowned singer whose decade-long string of releases had repeatedly held the number-one position and set new records for sales. Sought after and idolized by adoring fans around the world, Antonio Carrera had one day quietly stopped recording, while everything he'd ever released went gold and then platinum, and then beyond. And while skeptics across the country spoke of him waiting for the right offer, and music promoters offered the singing star millions of dollars to return to the studio, Antonio Carrera had remained in retirement, unwilling to perform or record or even discuss a deal that would pull him back into the public spotlight.

Until now.

Antonio Carrera, Arizona's most famous son, rumored to be living on a remote ranch somewhere in the southwestern desert.

Tony.

After the announcement, there was no chance of getting the audience to resume their seats. The party moved into full swing and conversations were drowned out as the musicians threw out a rollicking tune that drew laughing couples to the wooden dance floor. Everyone was happy, excited that Hands Across the Border had managed to pull off the coup of a lifetime.

Julia rose wearily from her chair and made her way through the crowd, looking only for a place to hide, a chance to slip away. There were too many people, too many voices, too much discordant sound.

She had fallen in love with a dream. *Her* Tony was a man who had built his life with his hands, raised his children with hard work, and wanted only the simplest of rewards. He was everything she had dreamed of, and despite her assertions otherwise, something inside of her had still hoped that everything might work out.

Now she knew that he didn't even really exist, and all she wanted was a place to lick her wounds. Julia wanted to go home to her quiet apartment, crawl beneath the blankets on her bed and stay there forever.

As soon as she was done crushing a dozen long-stemmed roses down her garbage disposal.

Rene appeared at Julia's elbow with her pink bow now tied around her neck. "There you are. I've been looking all over for you. I have some good news," she said. "During Frank's boring speech, I was talking to some nice young men and I think I've finally figured out a way to discover who your cattle baron really is."

Julia forced herself to say the bitter words. She'd have to tell Rene sooner or later. "Forget it, Rene. I already know who he is. In fact, most of the world probably knows who Tony is, and anyone less stupid than I am would have recognized the famous Antonio Carrera the second he opened the door."

"Antonio . . ." It took a moment for that to sink in. Rene shook her head, disbelief clear on her face. "No way, Julia. That can't be right. You have to be mistaken."

"I don't think so."

"Julia Huerta, are you trying to tell me that you spent the weekend with the sexy, gorgeous, eligible Antonio Carrera, the man half the women in America fantasize about?"

"I think so."

"And you didn't even know who he was?"

"Thanks for the support," Julia mumbled.

Rene laughed and didn't even stop when Julia turned and glared at her. "Here I've been feeling sorry for *you* all week," Rene said. "Now I feel sorry for *me* instead. These kinds of things never happen to me." She sighed dreamily. "Oh, Julia, I can hardly believe it. This is so exciting, and I'll bet it was love at first sight. I'll bet Antonio Carrera is just doing this concert as an excuse to see you again."

"He's probably doing the concert because he's getting paid for it."

"Don't be ridiculous," Rene scoffed. "The man has millions of dollars and certainly doesn't need our measly contribution. There's obviously another reason and I'm sure you're it."

Julia was beyond caring what the reasons were. She was tired, her head hurt and she'd had about all the celebration she could stand. "While you're thinking about it, would you please drive me home? I want to go to bed."

By the time he got Angela and Ricky to go to bed that night, Tony had almost reconciled himself to the idea of playing one more concert. Almost. Well, he had already agreed to do it, already signed the papers, but the argument against it was still a darned close thing. The final deciding factors had been Angela's repeated assurances of how happy Julia was going to be about him performing, and Ricky's take on how much money Tony could earn for the charity in that one night. Ricky was probably right about the money part. Tony didn't know what a clinic like Julia's cost to run, but he figured that if the concert were held in a big enough arena, Julia and her doctor friends would never have to worry about paying rent on the building again. They would be able to buy it, and the land, outright.

But, although there was no doubt in Tony's children's minds that Julia was going to be awfully happy about him doing the concert, Tony wasn't so sure. He didn't think Julia was the type to like big surprises, and he waited until the kids were in bed to make the call—just in case.

Damn, he was nervous.

"Hello?" She answered on the very first ring. Tony supposed it was too much to hope that she'd been waiting by the phone for his call.

"Hi, Julia. It's Tony."

There was a long pause, whole seconds where Tony listened only to the blood pounding in his ears.

"What do you want?"

He breathed in so fast he almost choked. It wasn't exactly the greeting he'd hoped for. "Well, I, that is I accepted, I mean I decided. . . ." Tony stopped, staring down at the receiver. A stutter he'd lost over thirty years before had somehow worked its way back into his speech. He shook his head and squeezed his thigh tightly to force out the sticking words. "I thought maybe, if it would help you raise money for the clinic, that I could perform at your benefit concert. The one this summer for Hands Across the Border. I'm, um, well, a singer, you know?"

"I know," she said. It sounded an awful lot like "go to hell."

"You know?" How could she already know? Tony had only signed the papers that morning. He'd thought he'd get to tell Julia himself.

"Do whatever you want, *Antonio*. Play the concert, don't play the concert—I don't care. Just don't send me any more of those accursed roses. The long stems tore up my garbage disposal."

Julia slammed the telephone down with such force that it surely shattered the receiver, and Tony winced at the sound. He set his side of the call down only when the calm, logical dial tone sounded in his ear.

Maybe the roses had been a bad idea. Women were hard to understand.

But Tony was to get his question answered after all. When he unfolded the newspaper later that night, he understood everything just fine.

REPUBLICAN CANDIDATE MAKES BID FOR DEDICATED DOCTOR, the headline read. The picture was big—almost a quarter page—and oh-so-cozy. It captured Julia leaning close to the senator. Her hand rested on Frank Leslie's shoulder as she, no doubt, whispered sweet words into his ear. Beneath the color picture was the question *Will a vested interest in Congress help clinic finances?*

Dr. Julia had a boyfriend. No wonder she didn't want Tony's roses.

NINE

The remaining six weeks had taken an eternity to pass. Julia had worried so much that by the concert weekend she had lost five pounds and her gray-and-white pantsuit hung loosely on her slimmer figure.

"You look fabulous," Rene repeated for the umpteenth time. It was easy for her to say; next to Julia's drab outfit, Rene looked like sunshine incarnated. Her long-sleeved blouse resembled woven gold and reflected a thousand shimmers of light, her pants were the brilliant scarlet of a jungle flower and her heeled shoes and jacket were a mixture of the two colors. Only Rene could have pulled it off.

Julia glanced in the mirror again and shook her head. Definitely drab. But how she looked wasn't really important. What was important was that the evening had finally arrived and would, thankfully, soon be over. Julia was worn out with the waiting. She was going to be glad when it was all behind them and they could get back to real life.

The week before, Rene had made the drive down to Buena Vista to help with the increasingly massive amounts of paperwork and ended up staying to organize the landslide of unexpected tasks that accumulated as the date of the concert approached.

The sheer magnitude of holding this type of concert was like nothing any of them had ever undertaken before. And, despite the constant hard work of everyone involved, the clinic's friendly, annual fund-raiser had become a nightmare beyond anyone's imaginings.

To begin with, no one had expected the concert tickets at the bandshell to sell out literally overnight as soon as the announcement was made, leaving the local folks in Buena Vista hosting a huge party to which most of them were not invited. By the following day, the mayor of Buena Vista had declared that the situation was unacceptable, and had used his mayoral privilege to move the concert from the hall that the organization had already paid for, to the rodeo grounds northwest of town. At the new location, the committee was forced to start from scratch.

The ensuing few weeks were a frenzy of preparations as the committee struggled with the massive task of changing an abandoned rodeo grounds into a concert hall that could hold thousands. There were concessions, lights, power and garbage to plan for. Not to mention ticket sales, bringing in seats and hiring a full staff to take the tickets and handle the crowd. Then, as the number of attendees exploded, there was also the previously unforeseen need to hire the entire off-duty police force of the three closest towns for security. The small group of volunteers that made up Hands Across the Border fund-raising committee were busy every hour of every day and no one had been spared. Julia had heard that Victoria Chavez was spending her days in tears. Giving up Rene during her busy workweek had been Julia's final exhausting effort. Now she was certain she would go to heaven.

So, with only a few hours remaining before the beginning of the concert, Julia resigned herself to the evening ahead and stepped into Rene's Sunbird for the drive to the show. At least there was one good thing about the crowd of people who were expected to attend—there wouldn't be any possibility of Julia running into the star of the show.

The streets in Buena Vista had seemed a little busier than usual when Julia had flown in over the interstate on her way into town, but the reality of the traffic problem didn't set in until Rene turned her car in behind the lines of cars already crowding the town's main street. The drivers honked and jockeyed for position as the line moved at a snail's pace for more than a mile. There, at the highway intersection the cars came to a standstill and the scene was complete chaos.

"I don't believe this," Julia said.

Rene waited about two seconds before twisting the steering wheel and sending her car careening onto the hard-packed dirt along the edge of the road.

Julia braced herself against the dashboard. Dangerous *and* illegal. "What are you doing?"

"I can't wait in that line; we can't afford to be late," Rene said, concentrating on keeping her car on the narrow dirt strip. She pressed the accelerator farther to the floor. "It won't be a problem to get inside," Rene said. "I know the guards, and they'll let us in the gates if we can just get near them, but first we have to get past this traffic. I promised we'd be at the building before four o'clock and it's almost that now." She gunned the car over a particularly brutal bump and only the seat belt kept Julia from bouncing skyward.

"Promised who?" Julia demanded. "*¡Dios, Rene!* Why does riding with you always have to be so frightening? I think it would be a good start if we showed up alive."

Rene slowed her car briefly to squeeze it between the barbed-wire fence and a wide LTD, then she accelerated again, throwing up dust behind them, and curses from the occupants of the LTD ringing in their ears. "We'll show up alive," Rene said, "and on time, too, if I can help it." Then she added under her breath, "Although you might kill me when we get there."

Julia screamed and grabbed Rene's arm.

"I see them," Rene said in disgust. She waited impatiently until the family of rabbits had hopped out of the way beneath the fence. "You can let go of my arm now, Julia. Your little friends are gone."

Julia leaned back against the seat cushion and tried not to look at the road. "Did it go that badly?"

"Did what go that badly?"

"You said I'd kill you when we got there. Did the concert setup go so badly?"

Rene looked at her for so long that Julia reached over to grab the steering wheel. Rene brushed away her hand. "Would you stop?"

"Would you drive?"

"I will if you'll let go."

Julia sat back and thought about closing her eyes.

"The concert tonight is going to be a big success," Rene said, thankfully keeping her gaze straight ahead. "And I think we have everything pretty well under control. I guess we're going to find out soon enough." Rene pulled the Sunbird up past the final car in the line and Julia could at last see the long, silver gates. "Aw, damn," Rene said softly, looking at the gates, "I hadn't counted on that."

In addition to the long line of concertgoers awaiting entrance, dozens of blue-uniformed officers patrolled the crowd, providing security, and also holding back what was surely the complete press corps of every major city in the western United States, and many from far beyond. Intrepid reporters edged their way through the crowd, jockeying for position near the silver gates, while photographers and cameras crowded the perimeter of the entrance, and long lines of wires snaked away to trailers parked nearby. When Rene's car was waved closer, the cameras moved in as well.

"Evening, Rene."

"Evening, Miss Rene."

The moment Rene pulled up, two young officers left the group at the gates and hurried over, practically battling for a place at the Sunbird's window.

"Well, good evening, John. Hello, Duane. It's so nice to see you again." Rene didn't flirt, Julia would give her that, but then, she didn't need to. The grins on the faces of the young policemen showed that just the fact that she spoke to them was enough. "Is it going to be a problem for us to get inside the gates?" Rene asked. "There seem to be an awful lot of people with cameras blocking our way."

"Don't you worry, Miss Rene," the tall officer assured her. "You can count on us to take good care of you. I promise we'll get you in with no problems."

The man's reward was a smile that made the second officer sigh enviously.

When the men walked away and Rene rolled up the window, she saw Julia watching her. "What?" she asked, all innocence.

"You are too much," Julia said, shaking her head. "I'm sure I couldn't get service like that even if I offered to pay for it."

Rene's expression gave nothing away. "They want to help me, Julia. They're just very sweet."

Maybe. But then all men were sweet to Rene. Julia had never seen anything like it.

The opening of the gates was obviously the first action the press corps had seen in hours, and they were anxious to be a part of it. Even with the policemen standing guard over the car, Julia's picture was snapped more times than probably in her entire life, and a pair of young men with microphones in their hands managed to outrun the officers and made it all the way to Rene's window.

Rene gunned the accelerator.

"Rene stop! You almost ran those men over!"

"I did no such thing, although I must admit that I thought about it. Would you just sit back and relax?"

Julia leaned back and clamped her lips shut, but she doubted she would be able to relax, and it wasn't only due to Rene's crazy driving. The moment they pulled inside the gates, it had become glaringly obvious that Julia had been kidding herself when she thought she would be able to escape seeing Tony today. Even if she didn't see him in person, posters of his sexy smile hung on every fence post, every tree and the walls of every building. Whether she liked it or not, tonight Tony would be everywhere. There would be no way Julia could avoid thinking about him. She would see him and hear him and be completely surrounded by his presence until the long evening was over. And in all that time, Tony would never even know that she was there.

Antonio Carrera basked in the entire world's affection. He certainly didn't need Julia's.

At least one thing worked out better than expected: Julia's first look at the new building for the concert left her simply speechless. After all the complaints Julia had heard from the committee about the accommodations, she hadn't been sure what to expect in the way of a concert hall, but she'd never imagined to find a handsome, permanent structure that looked as if it were designed specifically for that evening's concert. And with an overflow field beyond the building that offered inexpensive festival-style seating, the concert could now handle several thousand more people than was originally planned. "This place is an incredible accomplishment," Julia said finally, drinking it all in. "I was expecting . . . I have no idea what I was expecting. I just had no idea it would turn out so well."

Rene nodded. "Things weren't quite as bad as Victoria was making them out to be. When the mayor moved the concert, he had assigned work crews around the clock for a month to put up the main building. By the time I got here last week, there were only a few crews left completing the finish work and all we had to do was start getting the deliveries settled and a mountain of paperwork processed."

Rene parked the car under a big sign that read RESERVED and shut off the Sunbird's engine. She smiled smugly as she checked her watch; it was exactly four o'clock. A lanky, young teenager stepped out from beneath the building's shadow and waved.

"Another of your admirers?" Julia asked.

Rene raised an eyebrow. "A little too green for me, don't you think? Get your mind out of the gutter, Julia.

"In fact, Ricky is the young man who's been working with me to finish up all of the last minute details," Rene said. "He's been a big help to me, and he knows everything. He'll make a great assistant for you today."

"Why would I need an assistant? I thought you said all the work was done and that everything was ready to go."

"I said that the preparations for tonight are complete," Rene qualified. "But we still need people to work during the concert, too, you know. Stop being so lazy."

Rene stepped out of the car before Julia could protest that she wasn't trying to be lazy at all. She would be happy to work at whatever mindless job Rene needed her for that evening. In fact, Julia would prefer it. Working somewhere like the snack bar would keep her out of sight and help her to pass the hours of the longest evening of her life.

"You must be out of your mind! I've never done anything remotely like this," Julia argued. Rene had thrown the announcement at her clear out of the blue—as if she hadn't thought Julia would object to it—and then tried simply to walk away.

Rene waved aside Julia's protests. "I'm sure you'll be perfectly fine. You've worked on almost all of the clinic's summer productions. You're a natural, and besides, you're the best we've got."

"I've helped with little things, Rene, like children's shows. The worst problem I ever had to worry about was kids shouting in the audience. Even last year the board decided to hire professionals to handle the details, and that concert was nothing compared to this one. There's no way I can handle something like this."

"Last year the clinic's budget could afford it. This year is different and we've already spent all the money we can on hiring staff. Besides, I don't know why you're complaining. Everything you need to do tonight is going to be written on a list. For heaven's sake, Julia, you have a college degree; how hard can this be?"

"A degree in *medicine*, Rene. Not stage management."

The boy, her "assistant," tapped Julia's arm. "I'm pretty sure I know what to do tonight, ma'am. I don't think we'll have any problems."

Julia could already feel the noose tightening; she knew that she was trapped, but she wasn't about to give in. Rene's suggestion was more than impossible, it was unthinkable. "I cannot be anywhere near that stage tonight," Julia said. "Absolutely not. And you know exactly how I feel about this, Rene. You can put me to work counting change in the snack bar, or taking tickets up front, or even picking up trash in the field and I'll do it without complaint. I'll do anything but this. I am not going near that stage."

Rene walked away. "It's too late to argue about it, Julia. And besides, everything else is already taken care of," she said over her shoulder. Then she stopped and turned around. "Remember, we're all working together for the good of the clinic tonight," she scolded, "and now it's time for you to do your part. Just try to concentrate on all of the additions you wanted to build that the money from this concert will pay for. That should be enough to see you through."

She completely ignored the rest of Julia's complaints and even her threats. Eventually, Rene mixed in with the milling crowd of people surrounding the concert hall and was lost from sight and, short of tackling her in the dirt and holding her down, Julia knew there was no way she was going to get the woman to listen. Julia leaned back against the car. Rene was wrong. She couldn't do it.

"Um . . . Miss Huerta?"

Julia had forgotten about the boy. He would have to finish the job alone. "I'm sorry," Julia said, resting her head in her hand. "This isn't going to work."

"Well, actually, ma'am, I don't really think we'll have any problems. I pretty much know what we need to do."

"It's not that. I just can't go in there. You'll have to go ahead and do it without me."

"Oh, they won't let me, Miss Huerta. They only let me help backstage because I said I would be your assistant. If you back out of it now, I'll probably end up picking up trash in the field, too. Really,

Miss Huerta, this is my one chance to do something really cool. It would mean an awful lot to me if you would agree to the job."

Julia made the mistake of looking into the boy's anxious brown eyes. She could only imagine what it would mean to a teenager from a small town like Buena Vista to be backstage for the whole evening with a famous star like Antonio Carrera. It was probably a once-in-a-lifetime opportunity, a memory the boy would treasure forever. And he was going to need her help in order to do it.

As much as Julia wished otherwise, she couldn't disappoint him.

"All right, Ricky, I'll do it." Julia regretted the words even as she said them. "I guess I can get through this if you promise to help me. But if any messages need to be delivered to our star, it's up to you. Deal?"

The boy's smile could have lit up a city. "Yes, ma'am!" he said. Then he reached over and pried Julia's fingers away from the handle of the car door. With a nod of encouragement, Ricky began pulling her toward the building.

It had been too damned long since he'd done this. No, correction; it hadn't been nearly long enough. Tony looked around the rundown trailer that was his dressing room for the evening and almost smiled. It reminded him of accommodations from a long, long time ago, during the days when he and his dad would play their guitars almost anywhere someone would let them. They'd been broke a lot and living on the road, and a trailer like this had felt like a castle. Looking back, Tony had enjoyed those hungry days a whole lot more than the flush ones that came later.

He buttoned the collar of his shirt and slipped his signature bolo tie around his neck, pushing the twisted silver and turquoise knot up beneath the starched tabs of his collar. And when Tony at last stepped into his boots and set the dark Stetson on his head, the combination almost began to feel right. Almost. Then he made the mistake of looking in the mirror again and nearly called the whole thing off. But it was too late for that. Tony was going to have to face the music—and he was going to have to face the press.

It had already started at his house. Last week, the pounding of a helicopter blade slicing the air had shattered the awesome silence of the desert. No one had landed on *his* ranch; they had concentrated their search on the wealthy estates farther east, but they had been too close for his comfort. Tony hoped like hell that the interest was only temporary, that the world was willing to forget him again after this was all over. He sure didn't want to have to uproot the kids.

Thinking of his kids made Tony realize that he hadn't seen them in over an hour. He grimaced. Ricky would be all right; he had things to do and was good at staying out of trouble. But there was no telling with Angela. Tony could well imagine her leading a tour through his dressing room.

He heard the blow dryer going in the kids' trailer even before he opened the door, so he could guess where Angela was. Tony followed the sound to the bathroom.

"Hey, turn that thing off for a minute," he shouted above the jet-engine noise of the dryer. Instead, Angela and hair dryer spun around and the hot air blew directly into Tony's face. Tony reached out and held his daughter still with one hand while he flipped the bright red switch with the other. The noise and air stopped.

"Dad," his daughter complained, "I have to finish getting ready."

Looking at his daughter, Tony felt a familiar pain somewhere in the area of his heart. The black eyeliner and heavy lipstick she wore didn't belong on her fresh young face, and there wasn't a single wrinkle for the foundation to cover. After her day spent with Julia, his daughter had given up the blue eyeshadow and changed from brown lipstick to a soft pink, so that was some small improvement. But if Angela had her way, her straight dark hair would have been bleached blond, and her body clothed in lycra and lace instead of denim and cotton. Just like her mother.

"Where's Ricky?"

"Over in the building, I guess. He left an hour ago to set up your stuff. He's probably around backstage somewhere."

"It's almost time for me to go over now, too. How about helping me out?"

Angela was used to the request. She had probably done the drill a hundred times in her young life and actually set down the blow dryer without even voicing a complaint. "Okay, Dad, come on."

Tony went to the small square window by the front door and Angela crossed to the other side of the trailer where the bigger window faced the parking lot. "It looks good over here," Tony said. "Completely empty. Can you see anyone on your side?"

Angela mimicked his actions, parting the plastic white mini-blinds less than a finger's width to peer through. "There's no one yet. Wait! A big white van just pulled into the parking lot. It looks real bad, Dad; there's a satellite dish on top, and there are more vans like it waiting to be waved inside the gates." She let the blinds close. "You'd better go now. It looks like they're letting in the news stations, and once they start unloading those vans you won't have a chance."

Angela was right. It was now or never. And as much as he wished it were never, Tony was going to have to see the evening through. He pushed open the trailer's squeaky aluminum door and stepped out behind enemy lines.

Shading his eyes with the flat of his hand, Tony stopped under a tree at the corner of Angela's trailer and paused to survey the route he would have to take to make it inside the building without being seen. Without a doubt, it was going to be a tough battle.

His first mission would be just to get safely beyond the parking lot without attracting attention, and that part of the trip looked anything but easy. If he did make it past the parking lot, the protected world of backstage would be only a quick dash through the fenced entrance, across the empty field, into the main building, up the flight of stairs and down the hall. Tony hadn't dashed that far in years, but he was certain he would remember how the minute the first flashbulbs started going off.

He should have gone over there hours ago.

Enemy sighted at two hundred yards and parking. Tony watched from behind the old trailer's dusty red taillight as the gleaming news van found a spot next to the gated entrance. Now Tony knew he would have no choice at all; he would have to pass directly beside the van's doors.

Keeping his head down, Tony walked quickly to his first destination: an ancient, red VW camper that rested crookedly on flat tires where the chain link met the crumbling wooden fence. If he crouched just a little bit, the camper's tall windows made it a perfect vantage point to survey the rest of his route.

Tony wiped the perspiration off his forehead and resettled his hat for the next nerve-wracking stretch. He was almost one-third of the way to the gate he needed to reach, and now the only cover standing between him and his destination was a scraggly mesquite tree that offered little in the way of a hiding place. But today, Tony would have to take what he could get without complaining; the mesquite tree was destination number two.

He had almost reached the tree when the second news van entered the small parking lot. There was nowhere for Tony to run and nowhere left to hide as another television affiliate, the station's name clearly painted above the picture of the evening news anchor, pulled directly into his path. And two men had already emerged from the first van, bringing out three big cameras, and miles of snaking wires that rested in large, teeming loops that Tony would now have to cross.

There was no question. He was done for.

Tony began walking the final stretch to the entrance with all the enthusiasm of a man about to enter the gas chamber. The last two hundred yards would be a journey through enemy fire.

"Hey, Randy, long time no see. How are you doing?" The driver of the second van slipped a pair of sunglasses from his pocket and walked across the dirt to greet his friend. The two met in the middle.

"Bad luck," Tony muttered.

He veered to the right, stepping over a circular stack of thick wires. One of the men looked up from his equipment and smiled. "Afternoon," he said.

Tony laid a finger across the brim of his hat in greeting and increased his pace. The man hadn't realized his mistake yet, but he would eventually.

Tony was less than a hundred yards from the gate and beginning to think that he might make it when it finally happened. But suprisingly, the words weren't from either of the reporters or the keeper of the coiled wire. Instead, the shout of recognition came from the direction Tony had least expected. Straight ahead.

"Mr. Antonio Carrera! I would have recognized you anywhere. How exciting! I'm Victoria Chavez, with the Hands Across the Border Summer Night committee, and I can't tell you how thrilled I am to meet you today."

The late-afternoon sun flashed blindingly against the woman's arm of jangling gold bracelets, and shimmered smaller reflections against the low-cut, sapphire blue–and-gold sequined dress she wore. Her perfume overwhelmed the smell of fresh air and new lumber, and the woman's long fingernails bit into Tony's hand as she squeezed it.

Behind Tony, all conversation, all movement,

and all noise ceased. He could almost feel the eyes turning his way.

"The other women on the committee are awfully jealous I was the one chosen to welcome you today, but everyone always says that I don't have a shy bone in my body. I guess they're right," the woman gushed. "But since I usually do all of the presentations because they don't want to anyway, I wasn't about to give up the honor of getting the chance to meet you. And you're so handsome, too! I told them you would be, but none of the other girls believed you could possibly be as gorgeous in person. They all said your pictures were probably doctored up, but they'll see for themselves soon enough, won't they? And I can tell you, I just can't wait to see the looks on their faces when they realize that you really are."

Over the drone of the woman's voice, Tony could hear the enemy closing in quietly behind him. He could hear the soft tread of sneakers, the groan of the cameras, and the slithering sound of the wires snaking toward him. Tony was ready to bolt, ready to run for cover, ready to try to get inside the safety of the gates before it was too late to get away at all, but the damned jabbering woman still had a firm hold on his hand and seemed determined to keep talking forever.

"That I really am what?" Tony roared.

It was a mistake. Like a light turning off, the woman's flirtatious smile changed to hurt tears. Tony cursed under his breath for his own stupidity in yelling at her and shook away his anger at the situation. It sure wasn't this poor, overdressed woman's fault that Tony had agreed to perform at this concert tonight, and it wasn't even really her fault that the cameras were now closing in behind him.

Maybe there was still a chance to get away. "I'm sorry, miss, I sure didn't mean to shout at you. It's just so darned hot out here, is all," Tony said. "Why don't you and I head on inside and I can meet these friends of yours in person and you can introduce me." Tony slid his arm around the woman's shoulders and gave her the smile that had graced a million album covers. It had the desired effect. The woman's tears stopped and she looked up at him with violet eye shadow pooling on her cheeks. Sighing happily, she snuggled against him, affording Tony a liberal view of assets he'd rather not have seen. Tony turned them both toward the entrance. He was going to make it after all.

He took exactly two steps before he heard the television cameras click on and felt the lights add to the heat of the afternoon.

"Mr. Carrera! How about an interview?"

Tony was caught and there was no escape. He would have to surrender to the enemy. Turning around, Tony pasted on a smile for the camera.

Julia glanced up and there was Tony, on the television. He was standing at the entrance to the arena, wrapped up close to Victoria Chavez of all people, and looking down the front of Victoria's dress like a teenage boy on a date.

"That is truly disgusting," Julia said.

Ricky looked up from the cardboard box he was packing and frowned. "He doesn't really like that lady," Ricky said. "It's just what happens sometimes. He gets trapped into situations like that."

Well, far be it from her to destroy Ricky's hero-worship, but Julia didn't agree. That sure wasn't what it looked like on the television. A handsome young man stepped in with a microphone and the camera zoomed in tight on Tony's face, cutting Victoria out of the picture.

"Antonio, the whole world is wondering what the secret is that's finally lured you out of your retirement and why you would choose such a small place to stage your return concert. Is it true then that you've been a secret benefactor of Hands Across the Border for years?"

And now, Julia thought, he'll steal the spotlight from the charity just as Frank had.

"Hands Across the Border is an admirable organization," Tony said, "and deserves all the support it gets, but I'm really only a newcomer to it. I'm sure Ms. Chavez could tell you more about the charity."

Instead of stealing the spotlight, Tony did just the opposite. He stepped to the side and urged Victoria forward, effectively placing her between himself and the reporter. It was a masterful move to avoid the spotlight on his part, but not quite good enough. A second reporter appeared on Tony's right, blocking his escape.

"Mr. Carrera, why would you pick a small town like Buena Vista for your comeback concert?"

"It's not a comeback," Tony said. "It's a fundraiser."

"Is it true you plan to turn Buena Vista into the next Branson?"

"Branson . . . of course not!"

"Tony, which starlet are you really here with tonight?"

"Is it true you were on the French Riviera last week with Madonna?"

"How do you expect this opening to affect your reconciliation with Marta?"

"Will you and Marta each have your own theater when the strip opens here?"

Tony's head was bowed against the questions. He waited, not answering, as the reporters crowded closer, each demand louder than the one before. When they finally fell silent, waiting expectantly, eagerly, voraciously, Tony looked up. "No starlet, no Madonna and no reconciliation. Good afternoon, gentlemen. I hope you enjoy the show."

Tony flashed his million-dollar smile, but this time Julia saw that the expression didn't quite reach his eyes. And when he slipped his arm back around Victoria's plump shoulders, it seemed more like a kind thing for him to do than a come-on. The reporters had snubbed Victoria, and now Tony was making her feel important again.

"I guess we'd better get going if we're going to have everything set up in time." Ricky reached up and pushed the button to shut off the television. He lifted the box of supplies he'd come in for and hesitated for a second just inside the door. "You shouldn't think badly of him, Miss Huerta," Ricky said. "It's hard to be a big star. Most people don't understand that, and he has to give them what they expect."

Julia felt a stab of guilt that this kid should be defending Tony to her. Tony truly was a kind and wonderful person and Julia knew that far better than Ricky; after all, *she* had actually met the man.

"I don't think badly of him, Ricky," Julia said finally, honestly. "I'm just trying not to think of him at all."

The boy smiled. It took Julia a minute to see it, and a little longer to understand. Ricky believed her madly in love with Antonio Carrera—just like every other woman in the world.

The problem was that the boy was right.

TEN

"This is a mistake."

Julia had known it right from the beginning, even before being confronted by the pages of scribbled notes written in some unintelligible shorthand. And there was not one, but three curtains that she would have to deal with, long red velvet affairs that were operated by a whole panel of unlabeled buttons. There was no question in Julia's mind that she was going to cause a disaster. She would probably literally bring down the house. "This really is a big mistake," she said again. "I'll never be able to do it."

Ricky patted her on the shoulder. "We have hours until the concert starts. Don't worry. We'll have it all figured out by then."

He sounded a lot more confidant than Julia felt.

"Okay. This button on the end should be for the third curtain, stage left."

Julia glanced up to watch the back curtain slide back into place and then she returned her attention to the label she was making. The label itself was actually medical tape from her purse, but the black marker Ricky found did write on it and the medical tape did stick to the switches. Getting the pieces to rip apart with her teeth was another story.

"I tore this one in half." She handed Ricky both white pieces.

"It'll still work," he said, smoothing the tape over the switch. "Well, that's it for labeling the curtains. Come over and give it a try and then we'll move on to the lights."

"The lights?" Julia's voice squeaked. "I thought the lights were someone else's problem."

Ricky shook his head. "Everyone's problems are the stage manager's problem. You'll have to know what those guys are doing, so I'd better take you upstairs and show you around."

Julia had tried everything she could to convince Ricky that they should bow out of the job and that having her for a stage manager was actually far worse than having none at all, but it had become increasingly obvious that the boy wasn't listening to her. It was also obvious that Ricky knew exactly what he was doing around the stage and that did make her feel a little better. Julia took heart that at least one of them would be competent.

She followed the teenager through a tangled mess of hallways that ran through the walls of the backstage area. At last they reached a narrow staircase that led to a light booth poised high above the ground, and Ricky gave her an impressive introduction to the spotlights, overheads and footlights. Julia listened, but she wasn't sure she even understood half of what he said.

"Where in the world did you learn all this stuff? I can't even keep up."

Ricky shrugged. "I've been hanging around all week, listening."

"If you learned all this in a week, then you must have a photographic memory."

"Well," Ricky said, looking uncomfortable, "I've been to an awful lot of concerts. I guess after a while you pick up the drill."

"There aren't that many concerts in the whole state of Arizona," Julia mumbled.

It was over an hour before Tony was able to escape from the welcoming committee made up of Victoria and her friends, and it was honestly a relief to get away. It wasn't that Tony minded spending time with the ladies; in fact, they all seemed like nice enough people. But for some reason, folks always acted strange around him. They seemed to think they couldn't be themselves, couldn't be at ease, and that he wouldn't be interested in hearing the little details of their lives. Actually, Tony liked talking about everyday life. He thought that tractors breaking down, dealing with stubborn children and the washing machine flooding the house were all good excuses for a conversation. But no one ever wanted to talk to him about those things. They only wanted to talk about Tony. And Tony knew enough about Tony.

Finally he had managed to slip away from the crowd of women by mumbling something about changing clothes and getting ready for the concert. In reality Tony was just ready to escape the ladies' constant chatter. It was time to lose himself in the vastness of backstage.

The resounding quiet of backstage was awesome. It was always the same, no matter whether the concert was being held in a giant city civic center, or was simply a one-night stand in a small bar. Tony always liked to arrive early, to prowl the stage before anyone else had set foot in the area. He liked to feel the silent breath of the building and to hear how the sound of his footsteps echoed when the room was completely still. Tony wanted to find qualities that made playing his music in a certain place different from performing anywhere else in the world.

Later, when the concert hall was filled with noise, and all the confusion of the day converged with Tony as the focus, he would call to mind those singular qualities of the building. He would try to perform as though he were performing to the room of the echoing footsteps, the room where he could hear himself breathe.

Tony's twelve-string was tucked, as always, inside one of the giant speakers that Ricky had set up on the stage, and the well-used guitar felt good to hold as he paced. Getting ready for the show felt so familiar, Tony was amazed that he hadn't missed it. Not once.

But old habits died hard. He settled back against the far wall of the proscenium with the red velvet curtain brushing his leg and his guitar resting in his lap. He needed to listen to the room.

When the door to the world squeaked open again a few minutes later, Tony pulled farther back behind the curtain, hiding, unwilling to be disturbed again so soon. Maybe if he stayed quiet, whoever it was would just go away.

"Here's the list of everyone you'll be talking to and what they do, just in case you get confused."

Ricky? Tony started to stand up and ask his son

what the heck he was talking about when he realized Ricky wasn't speaking to him at all.

"You'll be wearing these headphones. The light guys, the sound guys, everyone will be available to you across that wire, but the end plugs in next to the curtain controls, so you'll be pretty well anchored while the show is going on. And this on the clipboard is what we call the prompt sheet. I know it looks confusing right now, but everything you need to do is listed on it and you just have to watch the cues to get it right." There was a sound of pages turning.

Prompt sheet? Headphones? If Ricky was training a new stage manager only an hour before the performance started, they were all in trouble. Not that Ricky didn't know everything there was to know, since the boy had practically grown up backstage, but having an inexperienced stage manager almost guaranteed disaster.

Of course, Tony wasn't particularly worried about building a following.

"Do I actually call all of this out?"

Tony froze. He'd heard that soft voice in his dreams, and there was no way he could have mistaken her for anyone else. Julia.

Tony had spent the last few weeks wondering what would have happened if he'd met Julia before she'd fallen for that slimy senate hopeful whose face could be seen on billboards across Arizona. Instead, the woman he'd dreamed of had dropped into his life already committed to someone else and fate had played the ultimate joke. After receiving thousands of proposals from women he'd never even met, Tony had fallen in love with a woman he couldn't have.

Tony leaned his head out from behind the red curtain. Directly across the proscenium, wearing ridiculously big headphones and a frown to match, Julia Huerta was reading through the gibberish of a prompt sheet for what was probably the first time in her life. She looked confused and worried and completely gorgeous and when Julia licked her fingers to turn the page, Tony forgot to breathe. He knew that nothing had changed in the way he felt about her. Boyfriend or not, Tony wanted Julia Huerta like he'd never wanted another woman. And he meant to have her. For a night, for a week, forever.

Ricky was looking over Julia's shoulder, running his finger lightly across the clipboard. "See? You watch the stage and as the list under 'events' happens, you read off the row of instructions into the headphones and everyone listening does what you tell them."

"That's a scary thought," Julia said.

"Piece of cake. You'll see. You'll be . . ."

Tony knew the second Ricky realized he was there. Obligingly, Tony slid out an extra inch from behind the curtain. The guilty look that leaped into his son's eyes told him exactly how Julia had come to be his stage manager.

God bless the boy.

Ricky was stumbling over his words. "Now, as an event takes place, you want to black it out with the marker so you can find your place easy for the next one. Listen, Miss Huerta, I have to leave for a while, but I'll be back before the show. Don't worry about anything, you'll do fine."

"Leave?" Julia spun around and was jerked back by the headphone's coiled wire. "Wait, Ricky! You can't leave me!" Yanking the headphone wire from the wall, she ran across the stage and made it out from behind the heavy curtains just as Ricky escaped into the hall. Headphones still dangling from her fingers, Julia watched as the door swung closed behind him, confusion and panic written across her features. "What in the world just happened?" she asked aloud.

Tony grinned; Julia was right to panic at taking this show on alone, but he wouldn't tell her that. Besides, she wasn't alone; he would be there with her. Tony stood up and brushed the sawdust from his jeans. "I'd have to guess that the boy saw me," he said.

From the time Rene had assigned her the job as stage manager, Julia had known this moment would come: the moment when she saw Tony and Tony saw her and they actually had to talk. But Julia had thought they would be surrounded by people, surrounded by noise, and that the moment would be painful, but quick. She had never dreamed it would be just the two of them, all alone, and that Tony would look so much like, well, just Tony. Somehow Julia had thought he would look different now that she knew he was a star. Instead, his smile was the same gentle smile and his eyes were still full of humor. She wanted to step into his arms.

The headphones clattered to the floor and Julia bent down to pick them up. She kept her gaze on her hands as she wound up the cord. "I don't know why Ricky ran off like that," she said. "I'd have thought the boy would be ecstatic to meet you. He knows all about you."

Tony's hands stroked the polished wood of his guitar for a moment before answering. Julia watched his hand slide across the shining wood, down the neck, across the curve of the shoulder, soft across the belly.

"Ricky's my son, Julia."

Julia jerked her attention back to Tony's face. His resemblance to Ricky was now so obvious that she felt foolish.

Tony had the grace to look guilty. "I'm afraid Ricky probably thought he was doing me a favor by roping you into this."

That broke the tension; Julia couldn't help but laugh. "Trust me," she said, "Ricky hasn't done you any favor. And when I accidentally shut down the lights or close the curtains in the middle of your show, you'll wish me anywhere but here."

"Aw hell, I won't care what you do," Tony said. "I've had plenty of perfect concerts. This will be one to remember."

Julia set down the headphones as though they were infinitely precious, concentrating on keeping her voice level. "I guess you have had plenty of perfect concerts," she said. "I was certainly surprised when I found out that you're the famous Antonio Carrera."

"And I was surprised to find out that you're practically engaged to that candidate."

The damned newspaper article. Julia had almost screamed when she'd seen the picture, but she'd never dreamed that Tony might see it as well. "That was all a mistake, Tony."

Tony looked up. "You mean you've broken it off with him already?"

He sounded so hopeful that Julia's spirits rose. "I mean Frank and I aren't even dating, weren't even dating. We were just seated next to each other at the dinner and the headline was a mistake that somehow made page one of *Lifestyle.*"

"With your picture right beside it," Tony added. "It was difficult to miss."

"I'm sorry. I can imagine what you thought."

"The worst."

"Me too," she admitted. "When I found out who you were, who you are, I didn't know what to think. Truthfully, I still don't understand why you didn't tell me."

Tony ran his fingers through his hair, leaving the dark spikes standing on end. "Well, at first, of course, I didn't know who you really were. I mean, the idea of someone landing an airplane on my ranch during a storm seemed a bit far-fetched and I figured you were just an inventive reporter after a big story. And later, when I knew who you really were, I kind of liked the fact that you didn't recognize me. It was nice to spend time with someone who didn't care how many albums I'd put out.

"The decision for me to play the concert tonight came from my kids. They refused take no for an answer. I told them that we should tell you first, that it was a bad idea to surprise you, but they were so sure you'd be impressed." Tony walked over and laced his fingers through hers. "Ricky and Angela really think you're something special, Julia. And they're afraid that, left on my own, I'm going to blow it."

The last of Julia's anger melted away. "Somehow, I can't see that happening," she said. She brought their laced fingers up and kissed the back of Tony's hand, then moved the kiss up to his mouth, pressing her lips gently to his. The touch was everything Julia remembered and more: more honest, more trusting, more certain that this was the man she wanted to be with, no matter who he was to the rest of the world.

Tony's free hand came up to cup her cheek, his rough thumb running across the sensitive skin of her jawline. Julia shivered and pulled back to look into his eyes. "Maybe you and I could try again. If I manage to make it through the concert, that is."

"You'll make it through just fine."

"I don't think so, Tony. If your son doesn't come back to help me, this may well be the shortest concert in history."

"That'd suit me just fine, honey. It means I'll get back to kissing you that much sooner."

Since Ricky had obviously abandoned her, Tony spent the next hour going over the schedule for the night's show with Julia. Trying to explain the prompt sheet to her was the most fun he'd had anywhere near a stage in years.

"So you begin at the very top. When everything is ready, you call for the start, the houselights dim to half and what happens next?"

Julia concentrated on the clipboard for a second, pushing a long, curling strand of hair aside before looking up with a perfectly blank expression. "I have no idea."

Tony squeezed in next to her on the step. It was too small for both of them and he had to slip one arm tightly around Julia's waist to keep his place.

It felt wonderful.

Balancing the clipboard on his knees, Tony ran his finger down the list. "Okay. You call for the start. You call houselights to half, call intro to full, cue the curtain—which is you, of course, cue the spot, cue the voiceover." When he turned to look at her, Julia's lips were only inches from his own. They were slightly parted and looked soft and beckoning. When he spoke, Tony's voice was strained. "Which part do you need help with?"

He stared into her gray eyes and watched the crinkle of humor deepen at the corners. "Does what I want you to help me with have to be on this list?" The question was asked innocently enough, but it was a siren's call and Tony could do nothing but acquiesce.

He knew that he had been waiting for this moment since a dripping Julia Huerta had stepped inside his kitchen and lifted her rain-washed face from the towel. He'd known then that he could never let her walk back out. And now, at last, there were no secrets left standing between them and no questions except those that time would answer for them.

Tony traced his kiss along Julia's jawline to the soft skin behind her ear. She smelled fresh and clean and wonderful and he ached to taste her everywhere. "I want you to come back to the ranch with us when this show is over tonight," he murmured. "Stay the weekend and give us some time to spend together, time to really get to know each other."

In answer, Julia's arms tightened around him, holding on as though he might try to get away.

Not a chance.

"Antonio?"

The bright light spilling in from the hallway door was almost as rude an awakening as the shrill voice that accompanied it. Julia stood up from the step so fast that Tony lost his balance, and slid sideways from the step onto the hard, wooden floor. He landed sprawled at Julia's feet.

"Antonio? Oh, there you are. What in the world are you doing down on the floor? Did you fall? Are you hurt? Heaven help us if you are." Victoria hurried toward him.

Tony rolled over and got to his feet. No doubt, superstars were not allowed to lie on the floor. "I just slipped. No harm done."

"I certainly hope not," Victoria said, moving closer. "We wouldn't want anything to happen to our handsome star." She used the opportunity to trace her pudgy fingers across Tony's arm and when she looked up at him from beneath fluttering lashes, Tony almost rolled his eyes. Behind Victoria, Julia grinned and fluttered her own lashes, hands clasped demurely beneath her chin.

On Julia, it looked good.

"Was there something that you needed me for, Victoria? I have to get ready for the show."

"I told the girls I would check on you and personally make sure you have everything you need," she said. "In fact, I'm going to stay and help you all during the concert." She leaned close, and her last words were only a whisper. Her smile implied exactly how personal her help would be.

Willing himself to patience, Tony covered the plump hand on his arm with his own. "Not that I don't appreciate the thought, Victoria, but I'm afraid it's a house rule that no one is allowed backstage during the show. If I break that rule for you, there will be an awful lot of people who think that they should be here, too. No matter how I might wish otherwise, you just can't stay."

Victoria's lower lip rolled out like that of a pouting three-year-old. "I've never heard of that rule. And since Dr. Huerta is back here with you, I'm sure there must be room for me. I promise I'll stay out of the way and try not to distract you."

"Dr. Huerta is the stage manager for tonight's show. It's her job to be backstage. Besides"—Tony leaned his head close to Victoria's stiff hair and continued in a softer voice—"it would be impossible not to be distracted by a beautiful woman like you." While he was speaking, he was also leading Victoria inexorably toward the backstage door. "And I can promise that I'll be thinking about you and remembering your perfume when I'm home tonight."

"Oh, Antonio!" Victoria's squeal turned into the high-pitched giggle of an overgrown teenager. With a last flutter of her lashes, she allowed Tony to nudge her through the doorway and out into the hall. And giving Victoria one last, intimate smile, Tony pulled the door closed and locked it, leaning his head against the cool wood.

Slender arms from behind hugged him tightly, giving Tony back his roots, grounding him in reality. He turned into the welcome of the arms that held him. "What are you laughing about?"

"You handled that very well. I'm always amazed at your finesse."

"*She* won't think so," he said. "I'm afraid your Miss Victoria is probably used to having her way most of the time. And as soon as she figures out what just happened, she'll be back with reinforcements."

"You're wrong. What you did was masterful, and you managed to get Victoria to leave without any hurt feelings. She'll be repeating your words for the rest of her life, telling anyone who will listen how the great Antonio Carrera singled her out for attention. And I saw you do the same thing today, when the reporters caught you by the gate."

Tony grinned and shook his head. "Don't be too impressed, Julia. So far, I've only been cornered by a lonely, star-struck woman and two untried reporters from some local affiliate. Just wait until the real sharks move in—that's when things will get a little tricky."

They began circling before the show even started, and the first summons at the locked door was the one Julia found hardest to refuse.

"Julia? It's me. Open the door."

The knocking and finally pounding had continued for so long that Julia had learned to ignore it. On Tony's orders, the door was left unanswered.

"Rene?"

"Yes, it's me. For goodness sake, let me in. It's taken me forever to make it up to the door. I have Mayor Donally with me, and he wants to come in and meet the star."

Tony leaned in close to Julia, whispering his words against her neck. "Tell them I'm not here," he breathed. "Say I changed my mind and went on home." Then his tongue darted inside her ear.

"Oh!"

"Julia?"

Julia pushed Tony away. "I'm sorry, Rene," Julia said, trying to gather her scattered thoughts, "but house rules say that absolutely no one is allowed backstage until after the end of the show. Star's orders." Tony lightly pinched her arm and Julia slapped his hand away. "I couldn't lie to her," she hissed. Tony looked disappointed.

The mayor's deep voice drowned out Rene. He sounded anxious, desperate to get inside. "Please, Mr. Carrera, you're throwing away a great opportunity here, publicity other men can only dream about. In fact, this could be your chance for a big comeback. You can't just walk away from *that*. We've got dozens of reporters crowded outside of this hall, and more are arriving every second. We've even got helicopters circling outside. If you'll just agree to come out for a few minutes, I can promise you the coverage of a lifetime."

Tony leaned back against the wall and didn't answer.

Julia looked at the man that everyone was trying so hard to get to. Tony's hands were tucked deeply into the back pockets of his faded Levi's, his shirt was a simple Western cut with a hint of braid above the pockets. Only the turquoise-and-silver bolo tie reminded Julia of a singer she'd once seen on an album cover. When their eyes met, Tony raised his hands in question, leaving the decision up to her; he would be whatever she wanted him to be.

"I'm sorry, Mr. Mayor," Julia said to the closed door. "Rene made me the stage manager—"

She clearly heard Rene's groan.

"—for this important concert tonight and absolutely no one is allowed backstage during the show." Julia ran her hands along Tony's shoulders. "Besides," she added softly, for Tony's ears alone, "I have better ways to fill this man's time." She leaned her cheek against his hand. "And we don't want to build up a big-star ego."

"Who needs it?" Tony agreed, tracing his thumb along her lower lip.

"Mr. Carrera? This is Wayne Montros of the National Evening News." The familiar voice boomed through the door followed by repeated pounding. "Mr. Carrera, you must let me in for an interview. If you would only give me a few minutes, I promise to set aside airtime on the six o'clock broadcast."

Tony slipped his arm around Julia's waist and drew her with him to the other side of the stage, as far from the door as possible. "I can't wait for this whole mess to be over," he said.

ELEVEN

As the last sweet note melted away, Julia sighed, enjoying the way Tony's music swept through the building, blanketing the huge space and seeming to hang there forever. The room filled with thunderous applause, which Julia wholeheartedly shared.

Then she saw Tony looking at her.

"Oh!"

"Lights, Julia! Lights and curtain!" a voice hissed through her headset. Even without her giving the command, the stage lights began to fade. Somewhere along the way, the light crew had realized that she had no idea what she was doing. Julia stepped up onto the chair to hit the two buttons that would slide the front curtains closed, then raced her gaze frantically along the list on the clipboard, trying to see what she was supposed to do next.

"Open the curtains once for the encore," Tony whispered from the stage.

Julia found the place. "Lights three, four and five up to half, spot one to full at center on five," she said into the headset's microphone. She counted aloud to five, the stagelights came up and Julia hit the buttons to reopen the front curtain for the encore.

The middle curtain slid closed.

"Damn!" Now her fingers were shaking. Julia fumbled with the buttons, well aware of Tony's grin. Let him laugh. He had the easy part.

The front curtain slid open and the audience roared with one voice that crashed into instant confusion when only the second curtain was revealed. Then Julia managed to hit the right buttons and the audience roared again as the middle curtain parted and Tony appeared in the spotlight, his twelve-string guitar resting in his arms.

Ignoring the stool that awaited him, Tony drew the frayed strap of the old guitar over his head and walked to the front of the stage, effectively defeating the planned sequence of lights. Julia waited, not daring to touch anything not on the list, not having any idea what lights to call. Then Tony handled it for her.

"How about bringing up the houselights?" he called to the men in the booth above the crowd.

Tony looked out over the sea of upturned faces, remembering the thousands of concerts in the past and unexpectedly savoring the present. Moments like these were the ones that had made the years worth it and made all the hours on the road not seem so wasted. It was the people who had made him who he was and Tony liked to make it a staple of his concerts to bring up the houselights for the very last song, so that he could actually see the people he was singing to, and so that he could thank them for liking his music.

Tony looked out over the waving hands, seeking the individual faces, the people behind the ap-

plause. In his poorer days, Tony would have saved a
month to attend a concert like this one, and he
knew many of these folks had, too. Not the ones in
the front rows, the ones wearing sequined shirts
and thousand-dollar hats. No, the ones he wanted
to reach were in the less expensive seats that
ranged the back, the ones sporting shirtsleeve tans
and John Deere caps that covered sunburned
faces.

"Tonight," Tony said into the microphone, "I'm
going to end the show with a song I wrote with my
father nearly twenty years ago. If some of you know
the words, I'd be obliged to have you sing along
with me."

He bowed his head, waiting for the stagelights to
dim and the spot to come up, wondering if Julia
would remember.

The lights dimmed right on cue. His doctor was
doing great.

Tony let the first few chords of the song ring out
across the room. They hung for a second in the
empty air. Then the tension in the room swelled as
the audience recognized the tune he was playing,
and when Tony began singing, thousands of voices
joined in.

He lifted his song to those in the back of the
crowd and those people who had only been able to
afford a seat in the field beyond the enclosure, who
stood pressed against the fence in an effort to get
closer. They were probably the ones most like him,
the ones who ran farms or ranches, raised children
and worried about the damage a storm could visit
on their crops. Tony remembered his days of sitting against the fence.

His gaze swept the rows of raised faces, undeniably enjoying this one last chance to entertain them, this final opportunity to sing his father's song with them again. That they knew all the words was the nicest present anyone could have given him. Then as the song neared the end, a streak of bright light from an exterior door broke the darkness, a flood of voices shattered the cadence, and the rhythm of the tune was interrupted. Half of the audience continued on with Tony, finishing out with him the final refrains of the two-decade favorite, but the other half shifted in their seats, craning their necks to see the new arrival. The song came to an uneven end as a new group of cameras and reporters and screaming fans swept down the aisle, all surrounding one small, bleached-blonde in leopard-skin pants and tiny white sunglasses.

It was the darling of the movie screen, Marta Marquez. Tony's ex-wife.

"I can't believe she's here. I should have thought of it. I should have planned for it. I should have known she'd pull something like this!"

Julia's relief at making it to the end of the show without another huge failure faded as Tony stormed behind the closed curtain. "What happened? What are you talking about?"

Ten feet away, someone was still pounding on the backstage door. "Are you sure that thing is locked?" Tony took a step toward it and Julia grabbed his arm.

"It's still locked. I haven't opened it for anyone."

"Of course, that's not going to stop her. It would

be just like her to have her lackeys knock down the barricades out front and climb right up on the stage."

"What are you talking about?"

"She's here. I should have known she'd show up."

"*Who* is here? You're not making any sense."

"Marta. My ex-wife."

"Your ex-wife is here?"

"Yeah. Last I heard, she was filming somewhere in the Bahamas. I thought that sounded far enough away to be safe. Who'd ever have thought she'd show up in a little place like Buena Vista?" Tony muttered. Then he looked up. "We've got to find the kids and get them out of here. Marta just uses them for publicity and they don't need that crap."

Julia was struggling to keep up. "Are you telling me that your ex-wife is famous, too?"

That question stopped Tony's pacing and his cussing. Julia thought for a second that he might be laughing, but when he came close and laid a gentle hand on either side of her face, his eyes were lit with affection, but not humor. "Julia, my darling, have you never heard of Marta Marquez?"

Julia could tell that he wasn't kidding. It was mind-boggling. Tony placed a quick kiss on her lips. "I'll tell you the whole story later," he said. "But right now, we have to find a way to warn the kids. They hate it when Marta pulls them into the spotlight. Then she just goes away again and they feel worse than ever."

Julia looked from Tony to the single backstage door that still shook under the demands for admission. Since the end of the show, the noise had nearly drowned out the cheers of the audience.

"But if our choices for leaving are to go through that door or to go out the front of the stage, I don't think you'll get very far. And I don't think you can keep them locked out all night."

The pounding was deafening, making the whole room seem to shake. It took Julia a moment to notice when the shaking also began beneath her feet, but when the wood under her feet shifted slightly, she certainly felt it. Julia jumped sideways and nearly screamed as the wooden panel floated from its grooves and slid sideways.

"Dad?"

The dark head that poked out from beneath the floor was dirty but recognizable.

"Ricky?" Tony bent over and slipped a hand beneath Ricky's arm, helping him scramble from the pit beneath the stage. "What are you doing down there? Where did you come from?"

Julia peered down into the twilight where the cobwebs and dust showed Ricky's path. The trail through the dirt disappeared into the darkness beneath the stage and Julia shivered at the thought of what else was probably crawling around down there.

"You won't believe the stuff I found when I was running the wires," Ricky said. "When they came to put up the building, I think the construction guys just laid the stage right over the top of what was already here, and there are all kinds of tunnels and chutes that the rodeo used. When I tried to come back inside to help Julia with the show, I couldn't find a way through the crowd and finally I remembered the tunnels. I figured they ran all the way to the field, but I'd never gone that far, so it took me a while to find the other end."

"This tunnel goes all the way to the field?"

The second Tony asked the question, Julia knew what he was thinking and she should have told him right off that there was no way. Ricky was covered in sooty dirt, and there were probably a million spiders who called the darkness down there home and didn't want to be disturbed. Julia was with the spiders on that one. She hated spiders. There was no way she was going inside those tunnels.

"Yeah," Ricky answered. "And I think you're going to want to leave this way yourself, 'cause I have some really bad news."

"I know. Your mom's here."

"Yeah."

The two men shared a look of commiseration that made Julia ache for them. "Does Angela know she's here, too?" Julia asked. Angela was so vulnerable. She could be so easily hurt.

"Actually," Ricky said with a grin, "Angela's the one who saw Mom first." At Tony's expression, Ricky put up his hand. "It's okay, Dad. I was over by the trailer and Angela came and got me before Mom ever saw her. In fact, Angela's the one who thought of a way to get you two out of here so we can all go home."

"I hope," Julia said, "that the way out is not through that filthy tunnel." She thought she already knew the answer.

Ricky shook his head, looking just like his father. "You girls sure do think alike," he said. "Angela wouldn't come inside the tunnel either—she said it was too dirty, but she did send you something that might help. Wait here for a minute." He jumped back into the hole and disappeared down the path in the tunnel. When he returned, Ricky was dragging an Army knapsack in his wake. "Angela sent stuff Julia can wear to keep the dirt off her clothes," he said. "She also sent a disguise for Dad to wear when we make our escape."

Now it was Tony's turn to complain. "A disguise? You know how I hate it when I have to do that, Ricky. Anyway, I don't think that's necessary—" The sound of fists pounding against the stage door stopped him.

"They want you bad, baby," Julia reminded him.

"Yeah. And there's a whole lot more people waiting outside the building," Ricky added. "Like hundreds. If they see you come out, it'll cause a riot and that would even be worse than the news people."

"And a disguise won't do any good," Tony said. "There's no way to disguise the guitar."

Julia hadn't thought of that. "I could take the guitar out the normal way," she offered, although the thought of fighting her way through the crowd was anything but appealing. "I don't really have to hide from anyone."

"It's already taken care of," Ricky assured them. "Leave the guitar in the spot inside the speaker, Dad. I have someone coming to get it."

Tony hesitated. He looked from Julia to Ricky, obviously sensing that he was already defeated. "I'm not agreeing to anything yet," he finally said to Ricky. "First, you have to tell me exactly what your sister sent me to wear, then I'll make the decision on escaping."

When they unpacked the bag Ricky carried, it became clear that Angela had been searching through the trailers when she'd been getting ready for their little adventure. Julia didn't know who owned the place, but they sure had bad taste.

To keep away the dirt and spider webs, Julia had been sent a quilted lavender nightrobe obviously intended for a woman with no interest whatsoever in looking attractive. It fastened at the throat with three huge white buttons, bringing the lace-edged neckline up nearly level with the lace on the matching cap. When she first put it on, they all laughed so hard that Julia was certain she would never move again.

"This is ridiculous," Julia said, wiping tears from her eyes. "But it will keep off the spiders. Now it's time we all laughed at someone else. Let's see what kind of disguise Angela sent for your father."

The picture was one that would hold her for a long time to come. Julia had to duck her head to fit beneath the boards of the stage, but still she kept her gaze on Tony as he handed Ricky the bag and prepared to jump in beside them. She could hardly believe it. Antonio Carrera, the dark-eyed idol with the crooning voice, had been transformed.

Hiding his beautiful eyes were mirrored sunglasses that reflected a rainbow of colors from the cheap tape at the corners, and his short dark hair was covered by a baseball cap that sported fake, brown dreadlocks across the back, making Tony look like a reject from Generation X. An enormous, tie-dyed T-shirt covered him from neck to knees and his boots went into the bag to be replaced by an extremely worn pair of high-top orange tennis shoes. The only evidence that the real Tony remained was the dark mustache, but even it looked different in the new costume and added to the complete disguising of Tony's face.

He had agreed to wear the ridiculous outfit almost at once, and only the grimace as he set the hat on his head told of his distaste for the clothes' possible previous owner. Julia suspected that he'd agreed so quickly because she already looked so silly herself.

In the end, only the knowledge that the one thing worse than being caught would be being caught in her costume made Julia jump into the hole.

When all three were crouched beneath the stage, Tony lifted the loose board into place above their heads and the prison became complete, a twilight world of long chutes leading to nowhere. And the only way Julia was getting out was through the spider webs and the spiders that no doubt inhabited them. She shuddered and tried to think of something else.

The loose board was barely in its place when they heard a door slam and the sound of footsteps racing overhead. Someone had either found the key to the backstage door, or had finally taken the initiative to break it down. Either way, Julia could just imagine the disappointment when it was discovered that their star had escaped.

Ricky switched on the flashlight and they all followed the yellow beam into the darkness.

TWELVE

"Stop it, Tony."

"It wasn't me. It might have been a spider. They're all over the place."

"Yeah, right. It's not *that* dark in here."

"Would you two behave?" Ricky's voice was full of parental censorship.

Julia pushed Tony's shoulder and turned to follow. "One of us needs to keep his hands to himself," she said.

Tony slipped an arm around her from behind. "Not a chance." His words were a warm whisper beside her ear. In the weight of her clothes, the added warmth of the nylon robe, and the heat of the windless tunnel, Julia shivered.

"Come on, you two. Let's get out of here."

Julia was all for that, and Ricky and the flashlight were already moving far ahead. She pried Tony's hand from around her waist and hurried after the light. She heard Tony's low laugh.

"I'll be right behind you," he said.

She smiled at the thought. She certainly hoped so.

"Do you see those lights?" Ricky stopped so fast that Julia almost ran him down. Farther ahead, she could see a square of soft white light.

"Is that the exit?"

"Yep. It's the lights for the field outside of the building and that's when we start the real test. We have to make it across that field without Dad being seen. I sure hope the crowd has emptied out some."

Julia's gaze swept over Tony's disguise, from the baseball cap and long dreadlocks to the tie-dyed T-shirt that almost reached his knees and the ragged orange shoes. "There's no way anyone would recognize your dad dressed in these crazy clothes," she said. "He doesn't look anything like Antonio Carrera. Even without the sunglasses."

Ricky laughed. "Heck, this outfit is nothing. You should see some of the wild costumes we've fixed Dad up in, and the people still recognize him. In fact, there were some that were way worse than this."

"That's enough, Ricky."

"This one time Angela decided that we should get Dad—"

"Ricky!"

Ricky stopped. "Well, anyway, that night Dad was real embarrassed when someone recognized him."

It had been a long time since Tony had done anything as completely childish as jumping inside a dark tunnel to hide or to tease a woman about a spider on her shoulder. Maybe that was why he was enjoying himself so much. Of course, having Julia with him made the adventure all the better and pulled Tony into the lighter, ridiculous side of having to hide from thousands of fans. Surprisingly, with Ricky's help, they might actually pull it off.

Now Tony just needed to find his daughter and get them all home so that life could go back to normal.

"Where are we meeting Angela? Is she waiting for us outside?" Tony asked when he caught up with his son.

"Don't worry, Dad, we've got this all planned," Ricky assured him. "Angela will be ready when we get there." Tony waited, but that was obviously all his son was going to say.

"That was a wonderfully evasive answer," Julia said.

Tony squeezed Julia's shoulder proudly. He'd finally found the right woman. "You didn't answer my question, Ricky. Where are we meeting Angela?"

"Dad, we've really got to hurry if we're going to be on time."

"We are not leaving this tunnel until you tell me where your sister is."

Ricky hesitated for a full second. "We're going to walk out and meet her. She's pulling the truck around."

"What?"

"Don't worry. She's really good at driving. She's been practicing."

"What?"

"Well, she had to learn somehow," Ricky said defensively. "She's supposed to have gotten her driver's license weeks ago and you keep putting it off."

"After this, she's not getting her license until she's sixty," Tony grumbled. Then he remembered. "Good Lord. She was trying to get me to bring the Jaguar today."

Ricky shook his head. "We didn't plan this escape that far in advance, Dad, honest. Besides, I would never have given Angela the keys to the Jaguar."

Ricky seemed to realize right off that he'd said too much and he clamped his lips together. Tony decided that when they got home, the boy needed more chores to keep him busy—he obviously had way too much spare time on his hands.

"Is Angela waiting for us in the parking lot?" Julia asked. It sounded like she was trying not to laugh.

"No," Ricky answered slowly, shooting another look at his father. "Angela's going to drive the truck out of the gates and over to the highway and we're going to cut across the desert and meet her. That way, Dad won't have to go past the TV cameras in the parking lot."

"My truck will never be the same," Tony grumbled. But secretly, he had to admit it was a perfect plan—except for the part about his just-turned-sixteen daughter behind the wheel. That part was making him awful nervous.

Suddenly Tony hoped Angela had been practicing a lot.

The tunnel beneath the building exited into a short, narrow alley between two rows of tall bleachers. Once used for rodeo competition, the enclosure had been turned into a seat-yourself field for the evening's concert with temporary seating placed around the edges. The bleacher seats were all empty, but Tony could see an awful lot of feet still kicking up dirt in that field.

When they were ready to step out of the tunnel, Julia removed the lavender robe and ridiculous lace-edged cap and shoved them into Ricky's duffel bag. She'd looked hilarious in the outfit, and Tony had laughed as hard as anyone, but he'd appreciated the gratitude with which Julia had accepted the costume from his kids. The woman might hate spiders, but she didn't care about appearances. It was a combination Tony could live with.

He slipped on the rainbow sunglasses, and everything in his world turned dark green from the cheap plastic lenses. Ricky was walking ahead and reached the edge of the bleachers first, and Tony whistled softly in appreciation as he watched the finesse with which his son handled his sudden appearance in the field. Tony had always found that furtive actions only served to attract attention, whereas a confident person could pass unnoticed. Ricky strolled into the field as if he owned the world.

Once outside the tunnel, Tony was finally able to stand up straight and he tried to ignore the weight of the hair swinging around his shoulders. He didn't mind it so much anymore, but a few years earlier, he had been damned tired of wearing stupid costumes everywhere he went. A soft hand touched his arm. "Don't worry. Your own mother wouldn't recognize you," Julia assured him.

Tony wasn't about to disillusion her. He slipped his arm around Julia's shoulders, happy to be with her no matter what kind of clothes he was wearing. The loose sleeve of his T-shirt slid accommodatingly high on his shoulder, letting him feel the warm skin of Julia's neck against the crook of his elbow. Rather than release her, they turned sideways to fit between the bleachers together.

"Hey, man!"

A group of teenagers dressed in clothing very similar to Tony's huddled in a small circle at the end of the bleachers. The teenagers weren't exactly the kind of crowd Tony usually saw at his concerts, but in this small town, they'd probably had a choice between an Antonio Carrera concert and another evening in the Dairy Queen parking lot. The good news was that kids this age generally had no idea who Tony was, even if someone told them.

"Hey," Ricky answered the hail, and raised his hand in greeting. He veered to the right and Tony and Julia turned to follow. Just in case, Tony buried his face in Julia's neck as they walked past the group. Even he was surprised when it took no more than three seconds before it happened.

One kid stood up from the group and walked a few feet in Tony's direction, standing alone to watch him walk past. Finally the boy's slow walk turned into a slow run, as he hurried to intercept Tony on the field. The kid had a thousand freckles beneath his backward baseball cap, and buckteeth showed when he smiled. Disbelief and excitement were written across the boy's face and the combination went strangely with his Deaths' head T-shirt. "I know you," he said.

Ricky stepped between them. Tony let his arm slip from Julia's shoulders and turned away muttering about "some mistake." Maybe he could just walk away and leave Julia and Ricky to handle the kid.

No such luck. The sound of tennis shoes pounded on packed dirt and the freckled boy stopped again directly in Tony's path. This time, he didn't hesitate. "You're Antonio Carrera," he said with absolute conviction.

There was no sense in denying the truth. Beaded braids hanging in his face, Tony put out his hand. "Pleased to meet you, son."

"I don't believe it," Julia said. She didn't think even *she* would have recognized Tony dressed as he was.

"That sure was fast," Ricky muttered.

"Record time," Tony agreed, cheerfully enough. "What's your name, son?"

"Tom Dobson, sir. I'm a real big fan of yours, Mr. Carrera."

"Tom, this is my friend Julia and my son, Ricky."

The boys shook hands. Julia got a "ma'am." She smiled. Obviously, the boy no more belonged in the wild outfit than did Tony.

"We've got to go soon if we're going to be on time to meet Angela," Ricky reminded them. Already, the other five kids were following their friend over and a crowd would draw a crowd. Julia could just imagine the reporters getting a shot of Tony in this outfit.

Tony nodded and put a hand on Tom's shoulder. "Tom, it's been a pleasure to meet you, but you'll have to excuse us. We have a ride we need to catch."

The boy's gaze drifted to the chaos in the parking lot outside of the arena. "Excuse me, Mr. Carrera, but you can't be thinking of going out that way if you want to escape. There must be a thousand people out there," he said. "You'd never make it through the gates without being recognized."

"I think we found another way that will work," Ricky said. "We're going to the end of the field and cut across that piece of desert between here and the highway. My sister is waiting at the road with the truck."

Tom thought about that. "That's a good plan," the boy said finally. "But that desert is a mess of cholla cactus and it's really hard to find your way through it. You'd better stick with me and my friends. We'll get you to the other side."

When Tom and his friends said they knew the only path across the desert to the highway, Julia had assumed they were just being self-important, finding a way to stay with the big star a little longer. But after she climbed through the slatted fence and began following the boys down an obscure path thick with grasping cacti, Julia decided the teenagers were right after all; she probably wouldn't have found her way across the desert without them. The dirt trail they followed was practically invisible as it twisted its way along a rocky ledge, through a dry, dusty streambed and beneath the knotted, reaching fingers of overhanging Palo Verde trees. Ricky walked ahead with the other boys, using the flashlight to scout out the path, and Julia could hear their laughter as he described their great escape beneath the floors of the stage.

"It's good for him to spend time as part of a big group of kids like that," Tony said. "Ricky usually hangs around with me instead of getting to do the regular teenage stuff. He says he doesn't care, but I can't help feel like he's missing out on something important."

"Hanging around with you doesn't sound like such a bad fate," Julia assured him.

Tony squeezed her hand as they ducked beneath a branch. "I'm glad you think so, honey, because I wanted to talk to you about that."

"About hanging with you?"

"Yeah." It was the sexiest "yeah" Julia had ever heard. She would have agreed to anything.

"There's the road," two boys shouted at once, as if everyone else might have missed seeing the two-lane highway.

"And there's Angela with the truck," Ricky said. "See, Dad? She made it just fine." Julia could hear the pride in his voice that his sister's plan had worked.

"Do you know what you're going to say to her?" Julia asked Tony as they started up the hill.

"To Angela?"

"Mmm-hmmm."

Tony sighed. "I don't have a clue."

"It was a great plan that she came up with, you know," Julia said. "Right down to the robe she sent me to keep off the dirt."

"Wait a minute. That's not what you're supposed to say. Who's side are you on anyway?"

Julia looked at the smiles on Angela's and Ricky's faces, looked at them surrounded by the group of admiring teenagers and she knew the answer. Tony had great kids. "Theirs," Julia said honestly. "Without them, you'd still be trapped

backstage with Wayne Montros of the National
Evening News instead of being here now, lost in
the desert with me."

Julia and Tony watched the disappearing beam
of the flashlight as the group of boys once more became shadows in the desert, winding their way back
through the cacti to the rodeo grounds and their
waiting parents. Julia would have loved to have
heard the kids trying to convince their parents that
they had met Antonio Carrera and that he had invited them for a visit to his ranch. She suspected
that Tony's phone call next week would be the first
time they would actually be believed.

Inside the truck, Ricky and Angela were busy
chattering and comparing notes on the evening
and Julia and Tony were alone, for the moment, in
the darkness.

"And now?"

Julia turned to face him and smiled. "And now,
what?"

"That is exactly my question," Tony said. "Now
that we've made our getaway, where do we go from
here?"

Julia hadn't even thought about it. She and Tony
had been working together all evening toward
their escape, and the subject of what happened afterward had never come up. Most likely, she had
pushed it from her mind because she didn't want
to think about it.

Tony placed a soft kiss on Julia's forehead and
she leaned into his embrace and felt his arms close
around her. "All my things are in Rene's hotel

room," she said. "But I don't have a key to the room and I don't know how I'm going to find Rene anytime soon."

Ricky leaned out the truck's window. "Don't worry about it," he said.

Tony turned with Julia still in his arms. "What do you mean 'don't worry about it?' " Tony asked.

"Julia shouldn't worry about her stuff," Ricky said. "Everything is all taken care of."

That sounded awfully familiar. Julia looked up at Tony. "All taken care of?" she asked.

Tony shook his head. "Here we go again," he said.

"Buena Vista Airport, second right." Tony read the sign aloud, then glared at his son and daughter in the rearview mirror. "We're almost there. Now will you tell us what this is about?"

Still no word from the jump seats. Not even an argument from Angela, and *that* really worried Tony; his daughter had never been one to believe in silence.

"What is Rene doing here?"

Tony returned his attention to the tiny strip called the Buena Vista Airport and pulled into the parking lot. The airport was deserted except for themselves and one other car. The Sunbird was parked right next to Julia's Cessna.

Before the guilty parties in the back of the truck could answer Tony's question, Rene was pulling open the truck's passenger door. "Where have you been?" she demanded of the pair in the back seat. "I've been waiting here forever."

"We had a little trouble getting away, but we

came as soon as we could," Ricky answered. "We're really only a few minutes late. Excuse me, Julia, could you please let me out of the truck?"

Julia climbed out of the pickup and pulled the seat forward. "A few minutes late for what? What are you doing here, Rene? I thought you would still be at the concert."

"I'm bringing your bags, of course." With a flourish, Rene pointed to the pair of red nylon bags next to her car that Julia always used as suitcases. "And as for the concert," Rene fixed Julia with a hard stare, "I was pretty much out of favor after you announced that I was the one to put you in charge. I practically had to run for my life when you wouldn't even let in the reporter from the National Evening News. That's the last time I give you that much power. I think I created a monster."

"I'm afraid the locked door was my decision," Tony said as he climbed out of the truck. He had left the dreadlocks and sunglasses behind, but was still wearing the tie-dyed T-shirt. Julia decided that even the crazy T-shirt looked good on him, and evidently Rene thought so too.

Julia had never seen Rene impressed by anything. From visiting politicians to medical emergencies, Rene had always kept her cool. But when Tony walked over to her and the introductions were made, Rene's expression looked an awful lot like that of every other woman around Tony. Of course every other *man* always looked like that around Rene. Suddenly Julia wasn't sure she wanted the two of them together.

"It's so wonderful to meet you," Rene said. "I've always been your biggest fan."

To Julia it sounded like Rene practically purred, and the fact that it was her friend's normal voice meant nothing. "Cut it out," Julia snapped.

"You just ignore her," Tony instructed Rene in his soft drawl. "These doctors can be so bossy."

Rene gave Tony such a knockout smile that Julia drew the line and felt obliged to punch her friend in the arm. Julia had seen Rene win over enough men with that smile.

"Ouch!" Rene frowned and rubbed her shoulder. "What did you do that for? Tell me that you didn't stare the first time you saw him."

Before Julia could deny it, Tony did so for her.

"Julia didn't stare," he confirmed. "In fact, she thought I was a beast and all she wanted to do was leave my lair as soon as possible, through rain and storm and dark of night." Tony slipped his arm around Julia's shoulders, pulling her to his side, tucking the top of her head beneath his chin. Julia figured it was to keep from being punched in the arm himself.

"I only thought you were a beast until I broke the dragon," she said to his shirt. "After that, you didn't scare me anymore. Just how much was that dragon worth anyway?"

Tony laughed. "Not as much as you, honey."

"Hey, Rene," Ricky said, "did you bring everything I asked for?"

"You didn't forget my stuff, did you?" Angela asked.

Tony fixed his gaze first on one child then the other. "What everything? What stuff?"

The kids never even looked his way and Rene ignored him. "I brought it all," she answered them.

"In fact, you can unload my back seat for me. But the question is, where do you want to put it, in the truck or in the airplane?"

Ricky sighed. "I guess this time we're going to have to ask Dad." Julia laughed at the boy's despondent expression.

"I don't know, son," Tony said. "Seems to me you've been doing pretty good at making the decisions so far today." Ricky stood a little straighter under the compliment. "But actually," Tony continued, "I believe this decision is up to Julia." He looked down at her. "I suppose you want to take your airplane with you?" he asked.

"I don't want to just leave it here in Buena Vista," she said. Even knowing that Tony would be waiting at the other end of the flight, the words made Julia sad.

"Okay," Tony said. "I guess you load the airplane then, Ricky."

Julia spun around, hitting his chin with the top of her head. "Do you mean you're coming with me?"

"You don't think I'm letting you fly out of my life a second time, do you?" Tony asked. "The first time I had a heck of a time getting you back."

Julia squeezed him so hard around the waist that Tony groaned. "But what about your truck? How will you get it home?"

"Well, all the men on my ranch can drive a truck. We'll figure that one out later. Besides, I think the guys have been expecting something like this ever since I had that old runway paved."

"You had the runway paved?"

"And widened."

"It's awesome," Ricky put in.

Tony leaned down. "I had it done the day you left. I already knew I wanted you back," he said softly.

"I could drive the truck home for you, Dad."

"No, Angela, you could not. And we'll discuss *that* part of this evening later."

Rene wasn't saying anything, but she was watching them with a big, sloppy grin on her face.

"What?" Julia asked.

Rene shrugged. "Nothing," she said. "I'm just a sucker for a happy ending."

THIRTEEN

The airplane circled higher into the night sky, rising above the scattered clouds to where a thousand stars formed the canopy of heaven. Never before had Julia felt so inspired by the view laid out for her enjoyment. But never before had there been anyone so special to share it with.

"Will you teach me how to fly sometime, Julia?" Ricky asked. He was in the back seat with his sister and Tony's guitar.

Julia pulled the headphones down around her neck. "I'm not an instructor, but there are plenty of flight schools in the area. Maybe you could talk your dad into letting you take lessons someday."

Tony squeezed her leg. It was evident that he, at least, was not excited about the idea.

"Can I take flying lessons, Dad? Please?"

"We'll see, Ricky," Tony temporized. "First, let's see if we can get your sister driving a car without any major accidents—"

"Dad! I won't have any accidents. Look how well I did tonight. I made it out the gates and to the highway. I even made a U-turn."

Tony ignored her. "—then maybe we'll talk about airplanes."

"I'd love to learn how to fly," Ricky said. "It's so awesome up here. Do you see the North Star? I've never seen it look so clear."

"And it's hanging right over your house," Julia said. "Pointing the way home."

"Home," Tony repeated softly. "I like the sound of that." His hand slid up to the back of her neck and began a gentle caress.

It would only be a short flight to Tony's ranch. Above them, Polaris and countless other remote suns vied for brilliance in the endless universe, but Julia's gaze was centered on the land below. Her dreams had already come true.

The brightest star had abandoned the heavens and was waiting right here on earth. Hers for the taking.

ABOUT THE AUTHOR

A lifelong believer in romance, Diana Garcia is an almost native of Tucson, Arizona, and enjoys raising her three sons in the desert southwest. In her real life, she is a wife, mother, and computer analyst, but in her heart, she is always a writer. Diana would love to hear from readers. Write to her at 2004 E. Irvington Rd., #205, Tucson, AZ 85704, or visit her on the Web at http://members.aol.com/dianagar1.

COMING IN JUNE 2001
FROM ENCANTO ROMANCE

__TALL, DARK AND DELICIOUS

by Reyna Rios   0-7860-1226-9 $3.99US/4.99CAN

When Ramon Santos returns home a wealthy man, most of the town wagers that widowed restaurant owner Consuelo Rodriquez will win him back. But Ramon has never forgiven her for marrying another man, even if it was to save her family. He'll remind her that he never gives second chances. Can Consuelo wine and dine her way back into Ramon's heart? She'll have him eating out of the palm of her hand in no time!

__IN YOUR ARMS

by Consuelo Vazquez   0-7860-1229-3 $3.99US/$4.99CAN

Alina Romero is a widow raising her son alone. At her sister Tamara's wedding, she runs into Brendan "Suave" Rivera. Suave is a close friend of her sister's and is also raising a child on his own. Neither of them is looking for a serious relationship, but they can't ignore the attraction they both feel growing. Will they be able to fight temptation when Alina's sisters arrange a romantic weekend getaway?

USE THE COUPON ON THE NEXT PAGE TO ORDER